Dead

by

Katie Gray

Published by and available from
theendlessbookcase.com

Printed Edition
Available in multiple e-book formats

The Endless Bookcase Ltd
71 Castle Road, St Albans ,Hertfordshire
England, UK,AL1 5DQ

ISBN: 978-1-908941-37-4

9 781908 941374

Acknowledgements

'Thankyou's' to my dear husband Peter for all his help.

Thanks too to the family, Adam, Jo, Maddy and Max for their support.

Thanks to Lexie and Carmel and Chris for their belief in me, and of course my wonderful publisher Carl for his help and confidence in my abilities.

About the Author

Katie has always enjoyed writing, although mostly just for pleasure. A few years ago she joined a writing group, and shortly after wrote a memoir - intended mainly for her grandchildren (for when they were a little older). She entered a number of writing competitions and was shortlisted a few times, and wrote some children's stories, once again for her grandchildren.

This cosy crime novel resulted from an idea of her husband's (although the body count was not high enough he told her!).

She went on to complete a second novel featuring the same leading characters, and at present she is currently working on a third.

Her books are not meant to be other than entertaining - the events are mostly improbable, highly unlikely and thoroughly implausible.

Enjoy!

Book Description

Pippsy and Jack Standage are private investigators who visit a luxurious Cotswold hotel for a restful break.

Alas it proves to be anything but restful.

Within a couple of days a car with a dead man in the driving seat arrives at the hotel's front door. Despite some initial reluctance on Jack's part, the pair become embroiled in a series of occurrences, which include finding a suitcase full of money in the boot of the dead man's car and a bag of diamonds lying in the bushes.

The investigating police inspector is perhaps not all he seems, and a number of the other guests look suspicious. There is an attempt on their lives, and some very nasty people kidnap them more than once! Somehow or other they always manage to extricate themselves, but can they find the criminal brain behind it all?

Chapter One

It was our first week away for ages. My husband Jack and I run a small private investigation agency and as there was a lull we took the chance for a holiday.

We were guests in a small country house hotel, The Flowerdew as it was called, quite luxurious and rather expensive.

Our room overlooked the glorious gardens, and even had a four-poster. Plus an en-suite the Queen wouldn't have found shabby.

As for the cuisine (too exclusive to be called food) it was exquisite. This was only our third day and I could feel my waistbands already growing tight.

As we sat on the front terrace enjoying the late Spring sunshine a car turned in the gates. Normally I wouldn't have paid much attention, but there was - something I couldn't quite fathom.

It proceeded at a snail's pace towards the front entrance. I screwed my eyes up trying to see the driver, but the setting sun caught the windscreen, making it impossible.

When it finally ground to a halt, that was it, the driver was in no hurry to get out. After several minutes I nudged Jack, who had leaned back in his chair and closed his eyes.

"What's the matter with that car driver? He's been sitting there for ages," I said.

"Hm, what car, what driver?" Jack peered down. "I expect he's yapping on his mobile. The car looks the sort some hot shot city bloke would own."

I sat watching, it certainly was a long call.

After ten minutes had passed, Robert Jones the manager emerged from the reception hall, and ran down the steps to the driver's window. He tapped gently then tentatively opened the car door and leant in. He straightened up abruptly, looking appalled.

"My God," he shouted. "This man's dead!"

Chapter Two

Robert careered into the foyer shouting at the top of his voice, "Call the police, dial 999, send for an ambulance......oh lord, this is a nightmare, a disaster.....oh dear, oh dear....." his voice tailed away.

Jack said gloomily, "Our first trip away for months, and this has to happen. Why are we always in the wrong place......?" his voice tailed away too.

"I suppose we could go down and just see what's happening," I said.

We did.

Robert had collapsed into an armchair in the foyer, and was being offered various restoratives by Caroline the receptionist, Charles the maitre d', and several waiters, all of whom were talking at the same time. As the waiting staff was made up of a variety of nationalities, most of them highly volatile, the noise was deafening.

By now, a few guests huddled in small groups, were trying to reassure each other that all was well.

We approached Robert who appeared almost comatose.

"Excuse me," Jack began.

Robert opened one eye then closed it again with a groan. "This is my first year at this hotel. It was to be a real stepping stone upwards in my career. I was going to put this place on the map. Oh dear, oh dear, the board of directors will fire me, make no mistake."

"Hold on," I cut him off in full flow. "Because some guy pops off outside your front door, it's hardly your fault."

"Don't you worry about that," Robert said brokenly. "I had to fight to get this position, the woman who has the ear of the Managing Director wanted her nephew for the job. She'll find some way to blame me, if I know her."

"Well, we can vouch that you had nothing to do with it. We saw the whole thing. The car turning in through the gates then crawling up the drive. You're blameless." I tried to reassure the poor guy, but he was beyond it.

"Look," Jack said, "has anyone called the police?"

"I have," one guest offered. "They should be on their way."

"Right, now we mustn't touch anything in or around the car, so I'll pop out and organise something." Jack said resignedly.

"You, you and you," he pointed to three of the waiters, "come out with me, and stand guard. I'll show you what to do. Pippsy, you get people into the lounge, and see if you can rustle up some drinks or something."

I bustled about urging everyone into the lounge, and calling to the staff, "Find out what everyone wants to drink. Sharpish!"

My firm tone had the right effect, the babble died down and the waiters began to move among the guests, in more or less their usual professional manner.

My husband calls me 'Pippsy' which is a pet abbreviation of my given name 'Philodendron'. What parents give their child such a name? Mine alas. They were keen gardeners, and after having given up hope of ever having a child, were rewarded in their mid forties with me.

They were wonderful loving people, but had no idea how I suffered during my early life with that name. It wasn't until I met Jack that my burden was removed. I became Pippsy, and so I've remained.

After a while everyone had settled, all of us clutching a variety of beverages, and I saw a couple of the waiters swallowing a crafty tipple. Still that wasn't any of my business, so I looked the other way. There was a low buzz of conversation, and some of the guests appeared almost excited, as if they were witnessing a TV mystery thriller.

Robert seemed to have calmed down considerably, was that his fourth or fifth medicinal glass?

Jack reappeared and accepted a glass. He jerked a thumb over his shoulder. "The Bill have arrived, and are taking charge. They'll want to interview everyone shortly, so we'd all better sit tight."

Robert turned visibly paler and took a large swallow from his drink.

"I ought to ring the M.D. and prepare him for the worst," he said hoarsely.

"Just tell him that the police are here, and everything's under control," Jack told him.

Presently the doorway was filled, or seemed to be, by a very large policeman, who introduced himself as P.C. Jacobs. He assured us that there was nothing to worry about, and that his boss would be along any moment. "Meanwhile," he said, "just relax."

I joined Jack on one of the sofas.

"Did you get a look at the victim?" I whispered.

Jack nodded, then out of the side of his mouth he muttered, "I could be wrong, but it looks a bit suspicious to me. There wasn't a mark on the guy that I could see, BUT, and it is a very big but, his eyes were wide open and he looked terrified. How about that?"

"What d'you mean, terrified?" I asked.

"Just what I say. As if he'd seen something that scared the pants off him."

"You think it could have been murder?" I said.

"Could be," Jack answered. "Either that, or he saw something that literally frightened him to death."

I sat pondering for a few seconds. "Looks like we might be involved in a bit of nastiness then. What d'you think?"

"I think," Jack said firmly, "that we are having a break and a rest. Once we've given the cops our little bit of info we should steer clear. If that means changing hotels, so be it."

He noticed my expression. "Now don't start," he said. "I know you, you want to shove your oar in and have a go at solving the crime. If crime there was, that is."

I said nothing to this. I knew that Jack's curiosity would get the better of him in the end. It always did, and we'd be off and running. 'Four Eyes Everywhere' we call our agency and I would say we're pretty good.

Most people think we're a strange match. Jack is tall, lean and quite fanciable. I, on the other hand, am small with a tendency to put on weight. I sport a mass of blondish curly hair, which looks like a floor mop sometimes. Anyone meeting us for the first time must wonder what Jack ever saw in me, I wonder myself on occasions.

We met when we were working for a large Insurance Company. Both of us were Accident Investigators. We enjoyed our work, but it wasn't as fulfilling as it could have been, so we decided to strike out as P.I.s, and we've done very well.

"Dead on Arrival
"

Chapter Three

We all downed more drinks, and sat waiting for further developments in the shape of the police.

By this time Robert's eyes were closed and his chest rose and fell gently. Surely he couldn't be asleep? Although considering the amount of alcohol he'd consumed, it was not without the bounds of possibility, I thought.

At last P.C. Jacobs's boss appeared. He was a mature man, thin, almost to the point of emaciation.

He introduced himself, "I'm Inspector Collins. I understand that some kind of unfortunate incident has occurred. Now, who is the manager of this establishment?"

We all waited for Robert to respond. His chest continued to rise and fall, but answer came there none.

After a minute Jack stood up and introduced himself. "I'm just a guest here," he said, "but my wife and I witnessed the arrival of the car containing the er...er... gentleman."

Jack pointed to Robert and said, "Robert is the manager, but I fancy the shock of finding a corpse on his doorstep has rather unnerved him. I'm sure he'll recover himself shortly, but if we can be of any help?"

"That would be most appreciated, sir," the Inspector said. "Is there somewhere a little more private where we can talk?"

"There's the office," Caroline said. "It's just behind the reception desk. Would that do?"

So that was where we finished up. A bit cramped to be sure, but adequate enough, I supposed. We seated ourselves, and the Inspector leaned back in his chair, placed his hands together, fingertips touching and said, "Now sir, madam, if I could have your names."

Having supplied this information, we then attempted to give a brief sketch of what we had seen. Which of course, was not that much. Inspector Collins however, appeared satisfied.

"And to the best of your knowledge, this gentleman was not a guest at the hotel?"

We assured him of that.

"But," Jack said, "there's every chance that he was about to check in, don't you think? Or why would he be coming down the drive?"

"Well now sir, that's something we'll have to establish with Mr. er, er, the manager, when he has recovered himself."

He nodded to us and stood up. But I wasn't about to let him get away so easily. Despite Jack pulling the most horrendous faces at me behind the Inspector's back, I said, "My husband saw the victim briefly, and he, that is we, think that foul play is indicated."

The Inspector stood looking at us, then smiled, rather patronisingly I thought, and said, "That is something that need not concern you, my dear young lady." (I just hate it when someone says that to me). But willy nilly we were ushered out of the office.

Once we were alone outside Jack snapped, "Why did you have to say anything? Now even if we want to explore possibilities, we're going to be marked. Make no mistake about it."

I poked my tongue out. "You and I can get round that. We've always managed in the past. Now, let's see if we can work out what could have happened to the poor bloke."

We went up to our room, and stretched out on the bed. Talking through what we'd seen didn't produce any startling ideas.

Jack leaped off the bed, and grabbed a pad and pencil.

"What we have to do Pippsy, is write down the sequence, as we remember it. It worked before, on that case where the couple had a go at bumping each other off. D'you recall it? She reckoned she'd been knocked unconscious, and he swore he was cleaning the car. Then he said she'd put something in his dinner, and she said she was at her yoga class."

I thought for a minute, trying to bring their faces to mind. A nasty couple I seemed to remember. We'd written down everything each one told us and looked for any flaws in what had been said. Finally, we realised their marriage was a series of fights and reconciliations, and neither of them were serious about committing murder. They just spiced up their love life! But we would never have sorted that out if we hadn't written everything down.

If memory serves, I think they finished up having twin boys and moving to a barn conversion in the country somewhere. What a pair!

So, we sat with our pad and pencil and wrote down everything we could think of.

As I'd seen the car making its way down the drive, I wracked my brain to picture exactly how it was. Sitting with closed eyes I watched the car turn in at the gate, then roll gently over the ground. Now what had I seen that could help? No, there was nothing.

The car kept rolling gently over the gravel. Back to the gate. No, the car just turned in and...... I sat bolt upright. What had I seen, there was something? It hadn't registered at the time, but now........ what was it?

Jack looked at me. "Had one of your flashes?" he asked.

I shook my head. "There's something, just as the car was coming through the gate. I just can't quite get a handle on it. Oh, blow, what was it?"

Then it hit me. "Yes, yes, I saw someone behind the car. Can't be sure if it was a man or woman, but they looked as if they had just given it a push. I'm certain that's what it was. Yes, the more I think about it the more sure I am. But where could they have gone, that road is very out of the way, and there are no houses close by?"

"Could have had a car stashed somewhere," Jack said thoughtfully. "But then," he went on, "that road is so narrow there's only passing places, nowhere to park. I think we're onto something, though God only knows what."

Chapter Four

Eventually, about an hour late, dinner was announced. To say that it was not quite up to the usual standard would be a slight understatement. In fact, it was pretty awful.

Jack and I left most of both the starter and the main course. As the dessert offered was just fruit or cheese, there wasn't much that could go wrong, but we only nibbled on a few grapes and a sliver of Wensleydale.

Unsurprisingly, most of us were somewhat less than hungry, but there was a couple from up north somewhere who always tucked into everything. Although, even they had a moan about the main course, which was supposed to be Filet de boeuf en croute.

The boeuf was as tough as leather, and the croute could have doubled as kitchen paper. As for the vegetables – well, I've never cared for mushy peas, so mushy broccoli and baby carrots were more than I could take. Plus, roast potatoes that would have stoked the firebox of a steam engine very nicely.

We polished off a palatable bottle of Cabernet though, which put a rosier hue on things, and as the level of noise around us rose steadily, the majority of the other guests must have been of the same mind.

Apparently, poor Robert had been assisted up to bed by two of the waiters, without ever having spoken to Inspector Collins.

Most of us staggered off to our rooms, immediately after dinner. There were only a couple of stalwarts, who repaired to the bar for their customary 'nightcaps'.

Jack and I fell into bed. My head was spinning, and not just from the wine and the quantity of alcohol I'd consumed earlier. The more I thought about it, the more convinced I became that the figure I'd spotted behind the car had been pushing it. I remembered thinking at the time that something was 'off''.

"Jack," I said, to the back of his supine head.

He responded with a groan. "Whaaaaat," he replied blearily.

"I'm going down to the main gate, first thing tomorrow," I told him. "I've got a feeling that there'll be a clue or two there."

"It'll be first thing today," he answered, "seeing as it's half past one. Now get to sleep woman."

I lay there, certain that I wouldn't get a wink.

Next thing I knew, it was eight o'clock. The Anvil Chorus was playing in my head, and my mouth was as dry as a cream cracker.

I sat up carefully, and waited for the room to settle down. "Slow and steady does it," I told myself. "A shower, that's the thing."

Well, I made it to the shower, but it was only by a superhuman effort of will. It was, however, the right thing to do. I felt, if not exactly better, at least a little less like one of Dracula's victims.

Jack was just visible above the bedclothes - dead to the world.

Whoops! Dodgy expression, considering.......

I tiptoed around dressing. Finally I crept through the door, closing it gently.

The hotel was very quiet for verging on nine o'clock. Not altogether surprising, I thought, considering the events of the previous evening.

Someone must have been up and about however, as the main door was unlocked, and faint sounds could be heard from the direction of the kitchen.

The idea of breakfast I swiftly dismissed from my mind, due to an uncomfortable sensation in my stomach.

I eased myself into the fresh air and sniffed in a large lungful. My head swam alarmingly, but I managed to stay upright. As I ventured carefully down the front steps, I noticed that the victim's car was still on the drive, albeit surrounded by police tapes.

Well, I thought, there's no one around, so why not have a quick peep inside.

I'd taken the precaution of bringing gloves, but even so I was surprised to find the driver's door unlocked.

I poked about gingerly, looking for anything which might appear out of place. Of course, there wasn't a thing. The police had obviously done a thorough search the night before. Still, I said to myself, there just might have been a clue of some kind.

That is, if I knew what a clue was supposed to look like.

After five minutes I gave up and closed the door. I eased round to the back and opened the boot.

To my astonishment there was a designer suitcase, side by side with a couple of matching carry-alls.

Surely the police couldn't have missed this lot. It was inconceivable!

Well, nothing ventured and all that. I tried the suitcase locks. No joy, the locks were locked. I had a go at one of the bags. Nothing doing there either.

That could explain why the police had left them 'in situ'. Chances were, they'd be back pronto with a locksmith.

I thought hard for a moment. I've got a little box of tricks that no self-respecting PI should be without, but, unfortunately, that was in my suitcase, which was tucked into the wardrobe upstairs.

Well, standing here wouldn't hack it, so I got back to our room as fast as I could.

I tried to be quiet opening the wardrobe and the suitcase, and I gave Jack a few anxious glances, but he'd all but disappeared under the bedclothes by this time.

The little wallet was tucked away in a pocket at the bottom of the case. I didn't bother to put the case back in the wardrobe, I concerned myself with getting quietly out of the room.

Although nothing was happening outside, I did feel uncomfortable opening the suitcase.

My jaw didn't just drop, it almost fell off. The case was full to the brim with bundles of fifty pound notes.

Gordon Bennett! I just stood there gawping. Then almost on autopilot, I shut the case.

If the case was full of money, what was in the bags? I couldn't resist.

They proved however, to be a disappointment. Full to the brim yes, but one contained only immaculately laundered shirts and underwear, and the other, laundry yet to be immaculatised!

Probably no such word, I thought, but it seemed appropriate.

I closed the bags then about to shut the boot lid, I stopped. Could there, possibly, be something which would reveal the identity of the deceased?

Very carefully I riffled through both the dirty and clean contents of the bags. Nothing.

That left the suitcase. For some reason I was reluctant to look through that. Still, needs must, I supposed.

There it lay in all its glory. Bundles and bundles of it. Filthy lucre, dibs, wonga, whatever you wanted to call it. I gingerly picked up one bundle. There must have been at least a hundred notes there.

I delved to the bottom of the case, fingers scrabbling around. Then I felt something which was not a bundle of notes. Trying not to disturb the contents, I eased into a view a small red covered notebook.

I stood for a few seconds holding it then it was all action. I smoothed the bundles down, closed the suitcase, locked it and shut the boot lid.

Hangovers and queasy stomachs forgotten, I took off back to our room, like a rocket.

Jack was still out for the count, when I stumbled in. I just collapsed onto the bed and lay there, gasping.

Gradually I calmed down, and my brain began to function. The notebook felt as if it was burning a hole in the palm of my hand, but somehow I couldn't bring myself to open it yet.

This was something Jack and I must do together.

I rolled over and lifted the duvet.

"Jack," I whispered. "Wake up."

No answer.

"Jack, hon," I tried a little louder.

I might have been talking to a waxwork.

"Jack!" I hollered at last.

"Whaa, whaa...what the hell's happened?" He finally surfaced.

He looked even worse than I'd felt earlier. Eyes barely open, mouth opening and closing like a goldfish in a bowl, he peered in my direction.

"Jack!" I could have shaken him, but I didn't have the heart – he looked so awful.

He managed to struggle into a sitting position, groaning and moaning.

"What's goin' on. Oh God, I feel like death. I can't hold my booze like I used to. How come you're not suffering? My head's left my body. It's got to be around here somewhere..."

He was chuntering on as if his brain had left his skull.

In desperation, I filled a glass with water from the bottle by the bed, and poured it over his head. It pulled him together quite quickly, even if the words uttering from between his lips would have been a series of asterisks when printed.

"Shut up!" I told him briskly, "and listen to me. I've been down to that car, and had a look in the boot. There's luggage in there. It was locked, but I got it open with my box of tricks, and just look at what I found."

I held the notebook up triumphantly.

An expression of complete horror came over his face.

"Pippsy, you didn't. Did you? Oh, my godfathers, please tell me you didn't."

I nodded, grinning. "I sure did," I said, "but I haven't opened it yet. I thought we could do that together. It's only right and proper, seeing as we're a team."

He looked as if he was going to throw up.

"There's nothing to worry about," I told him blithely. "Nobody saw me, plus I'm wearing gloves. I mean, worse comes to worst, we can pretend we found this in the bushes."

Jack groaned again, and fell back on his pillow.

"What am I married to? You're always doing this sort of thing. Remember what that CID bloke told us last time, and I quote, 'Keep your noses out of police business'. You'll land us both in deep poo one of these days."

But I was off and running. "I reckon this book's going to provide all the clues we need, to find out what happened to that bloke."

Carefully almost daintily, I opened the book and stared at the first page. What I saw was a list of days, numbers and times.

I turned the page. More days and times.

At least I supposed they were days and times.

"Well, hon," I said, "it's hardly going to make the best seller list, but to someone I'm sure it would make an interesting read."

Despite his reluctance, Jack couldn't resist. He sat up again and peered over my shoulder. We sat, turning page after page. Finally we came to the end, and were no wiser than when we began.

"Could these be days and times of meetings?" I wondered.

"No," Jack said, wrinkling his forehead in concentration. "Some of the times overlap. Look here, it says Tuesday, 130, 10.00-11.00 a.m. D.M. But the next one is 137, 10.00-12 noon. L.a O. So, it could be anything."

I nodded glumly, he was right of course – there wasn't the slightest clue as to what was meant.

Jack pushed back the duvet, and carefully swung his legs out of bed. Holding tightly to the headboard, he levered himself to his feet.

"Whew", he said, "is the room really rocking up and down?"

"Yeah, if you like," I answered. "Go and shower, it did me a world of good."

Staggering slightly he made his way into the en-suite and after a minute of two I heard the sound of the shower. This morning, however, his usual rendition of "Nessun Dorma" was conspicuous by its absence.

I stayed where I was, and continued to study the pages of the book.

What could this information signify? Train times or flight times, the possibilities seemed endless. The initials could refer to a person.

Jack finished his shower, and came back into the bedroom wrapped in a towel.

"I've had a thought," he told me. "Maybe, just maybe, it's delivery times for that dosh in the suitcase. Which would mean, this bloke was here to meet someone. What d'you think?"

"It could be wages, couldn't it?" I was getting into the swing. "Perhaps the money's payments for the staff here. Though as Robert didn't recognise the bloke, or appear to, that makes it a bit iffy doesn't it?"

Jack began to dress, obviously deep in thought. I stayed where I was, still gazing at the book.

"Perhaps," I said, "it's more sinister. Suppose this guy was making a payoff to somebody. For drugs or something?"

"Pippsy. I know you, you'll have some mafia godfather involved in gang warfare, settled in here for the duration."

I pouted, I do that rather well. "It was just another idea. There must be several explanations, and we've got to examine all the angles."

Jack put his arm round me, and gave me a hug. "You and your angles. You'll never give up will you, until we're both in it up to our necks?"

"You've got to admit that it's intriguing," I said, cuddling against him. "Tell you what, let's go down and get some breakfast....."

Jack paled visibly.

"Well, just some tea and toast. I don't think I could fancy much, after all that booze we put away last night."

"The trouble was," Jack said, "the meal was so lousy that we hardly ate. Just drank. No wonder I feel like the Twilight of the Gods this morning. You're right, as usual, tea and toast it is."

The dining room was very quiet. Normally there would have been a pleasant buzz of conversation, with guests greeting each other cheerily. Today, only three other tables were occupied, and those occupants were nibbling on either dry biscuits or dry toast. Even the waiters moved carefully, and smiled wanly.

"Nothing like a possible murder, and a few drinks, to sort the wheat from the chaff," I whispered to Jack.

We ordered a large pot of tea, and a slice of toast each. As we chewed unenthusiastically on the toast, I looked around at the other guests.

There was the couple from the north. They didn't look too bad as a matter of fact, but I felt sure that they were the last people to be involved in anything shady.

Sitting by the window was a group made up of two couples, aged in their early forties I guessed. The men were tall, good looking, and dressed in expensive casuals. Their wives, or partners or whatever, were carefully made up, and wearing designer dresses, exposing lots of cleavage, even at this time in the morning. Now there was a possibility. I studied them as discreetly as I could, straining to overhear anything they might say.

Yes, I would certainly mark them down as suspicious.

On the far side of the room was a family. Mother, father and two teenage children, a boy and a girl. The girl had the familiar sullen expression of so many teenage girls. While the boy lounged in his chair, tapping his teeth with a finger. Highly unlikely, I told myself. Still, count nothing out. The parents appeared to be arguing as to how the day should be spent.

I couldn't hear clearly, and was about to switch off, when the man said something that made me sit up.

"Jack," I said quietly. "That couple across the room, the father just said that he would have to reschedule a business meeting, after what happened last night. Could be something, d'you think?"

"I think you're reaching for things, Pippsy my love. Could just be that he feels as hungover as the rest of us."

"All the same," I pondered, "it might be worth keeping an eye out. Let's sit in the lounge and wait to see what they do."

Jack cast his eyes heavenwards, but followed me as I stood up and strolled in the direction of the lounge. I smiled at the family group as we passed. The children ignored us, but the father nodded briefly. The mother stared as if we'd landed from outer space. Maybe she was more hungover than we were!

We sat in the lounge for a few minutes just waiting. Presently the father left the dining room and crossed to the reception desk.

Caroline was seated, looking a little pale, it has to be said, but she smiled pleasantly enough as the man asked her for an outside line.

"Can't get a mobile signal here," he said.

There were one or two telephones on tables dotted around the reception hall. He sat down and picked up the phone. After punching in a number, he began speaking rapidly and softly into the mouthpiece. He paused, obviously listening. Whatever the response, it seemed to be less than satisfactory. He rattled away again, his cheeks becoming very flushed.

I did my best, but even my practised ears couldn't make out a word. I glanced at Jack. He was holding his watch to his ear, and looking into the distance.

The man banged the phone down and left in quite a hurry. His wife and children appeared a few minutes later and made their way to the stairs. There was quite a babble of chat coming from them. But the most interesting thing I heard was, "Let's get out of here, I'm fed up," from the daughter.

I turned to Jack and pointed in the direction the man had gone, "Wonder what all that was about?"

Jack gave me a sly smile. "Let's go outside for a breath, shall we?"

Chapter Five

We walked slowly up the drive towards the gate, I was babbling something about looking for clues in the lane, when Jack stopped me dead in my tracks.

"Our guy was in contact with someone who seemed to be asking for money..... and saying that nothing had arrived yet. How about that?"

"How....how did you find that out?" I was frozen to the spot.

"You're not the only one with a box of tricks. I was keeping this as a surprise. You'll remember I saw Benny Bradley a couple of weeks ago? Well, he got me a little gizmo, which I think is going to come in handy."

Jack pulled back the sleeve of his sweatshirt and pointed to his watch. I peered down at it.

"It's a new watch, so what?" I asked.

"Look and learn, my love, look and learn," he said with a smug expression. I could have socked him on the jaw.

He twiddled what I thought was the winder, and held it to my ear. We had passed a couple of ground staff earlier, who were sitting enjoying a crafty fag.

"So I says to him, I says, I don't want to hear anyfink more from you my son, or you'll get a bunch of fives to the moush."

I gawped at Jack.

"It's some sort of receiver, isn't it? Is it legal? Couldn't you be in trouble for having something like that?"

Jack burst out laughing. "You're a fine one to talk about legal. You and your box of tricks. I thought I could do with some help as well. Ben's done me proud hasn't he? Cost a bit of course, but worth every penny don't you think?"

I was still staring at the innocent looking watch.

"It's marvellous, and I mean no one could possibly tell a thing. Has it got a good range?"

"As good as we're ever likely to need. I tried it out a couple of times before we came away. I was hoping to get a chance to put it into practise." Jack was very pleased with himself.

I didn't know whether to kiss him, or thump him for keeping me in the dark until now.

By this time we were almost at the gate.

"Let's just have a quick gander in the lane, and see if there's any hint of what might have happened," I said.

We tried to look casual, just in case anyone was watching.

After strolling up and down a few times, without success, we decided to turn back. Then I spotted it, caught at the base of a bush. A small bag of some description. I grabbed it. It was made of dark green suede, making it hard to spot.

I just had to have a peep. There was a drawstring at the neck, and very carefully I slid my fingers in and pulled it apart.

Inside was a piece of matching suede cloth enclosing some hard objects. My heart was doing somersaults as I unfolded the cloth. I was not entirely surprised by what I found.

Several huge, and I mean huge, diamonds. They flashed and twinkled in the morning sunlight.

Jack and I stood gazing at them, with a mixture of fascination and apprehension.

"Oh good grief." My voice had become unnaturally high pitched.

"Good grief doesn't do it for me," Jack said, "but I know what you mean."

We looked at each other in consternation. Whatever had happened to the dead bloke, these stones must have been at the heart of it.

Talking of hearts, mine was now doing a good imitation of a steam hammer working at double time.

"What d'you think we should do next?" I was still squeaking.

Jack pulled his lower lip between thumb and forefinger. He does this when he's got his brain in top gear.

"Well, the obvious thing would be to give them to the police," he said. "But then, we'd have to explain just why we were out in the lane, poking around. It's going to dawn on them fairly swiftly, that we weren't out here by chance. I mean, you would have to be really looking for something to see this."

He held the bag up. "Dark green suede, four or five inches square, hidden in a bush? No chance we came on that by accident."

"We can't just put it back," I protested. "It's vital evidence – don't know of what – but evidence of something."

"I wasn't planning on putting it back," Jack said. "I think we should hang onto it until we find out how that bloke popped. It'll give us time to work out some story or other."

Jack's always told me I sail close to the wind, but this beat anything I'd ever thought of.

Acting casual again, we strolled back through the gates. Jack had put the bag in his pocket. Luckily his sweatshirt was capacious enough to disguise any bulge.

We'd barely reached the front steps, when a police car swung through the gates and sped down the drive. I discovered I'd broken into a sweat. A cold one.

Inspector Collins alighted and strode in our direction.

"Good morning, sir, madam," he nodded, with a twitch of the lips that I suppose, passed for a smile.

"Morning Inspector," Jack responded heartily, while I squeaked something or other.

Inspector Collins paused, looking at us, "Is the manager up and about today?" he asked.

"I haven't seen him yet," I managed to squawk.

The Inspector gave me an odd look. I cleared my throat, "Got a bit of a dry throat today. Must have been all the drink last night. Ha, ha, ha..." I tailed off into silence, as no one else was laughing.

He brushed past me and made his way inside.

We heard him asking Caroline if he could speak to the manager.

"Let's get to our room, a bit swiftish," Jack said. "Then we can take stock."

By the time we got upstairs my legs had turned to jelly. I flopped onto the bed, and groaned.

Jack took the bag from his pocket and sat on the edge.

"As I see it," he said, "these stones have got to be stolen. But if that's the case, and the dead bloke had something to do with it then somebody is going to be looking for them."

I groaned again. Something similar had occurred to me.

The 'somebody' might soon be looking for us, if we weren't careful. Suddenly, being a private investigator didn't seem such an appealing job.

"Let's just hand them over the cops, and have done with the whole thing," I said gloomily.

Jack, who was usually the cautious one, looked at me in surprise. "Never thought I'd hear you give up so easily," he said.

I had to agree. I never thought I would either.

What had seemed like an interesting game, though, had begun to look less like a game, and very dangerous.

Chapter Six

Robert appeared to have recovered somewhat by lunchtime. He greeted us in a more restrained manner than usual, but seemed none the worse for wear after his abrupt departure the previous evening.

Even Jack was not particularly hungry, but we forced down a salad. It was a big improvement on the previous night's cuisine.

There was an increase in occupied tables too. Most other guests were also opting for light fare, with of course, the exception of the couple from the North, who tucked into a starter followed by fish and chips, all rounded off with apple pie and cream.

As we ate I looked around at the tables. The man who had been on the phone was not in evidence, but his wife and children sat silently munching without any appearance of enjoyment.

Just as we were about to leave, there was a flurry of activity at the dining room door. In came a glamorous blonde girl, probably in her mid-twenties, accompanied by a much older – judging by his receding grey hair and jowls – stockily built man.

The girl was talking twenty to the dozen at the top of her voice. "So I says to him, you can't talk to me like that, my money's as good as anybody's. My friend could buy and sell your rotten place without breaking sweat, I says. Well, that quieted him down a bit, I can tell you."

She rattled on in this vein for a few minutes more, after they were seated. Her companion suddenly leant forward and said something. Just a few words. The girl stopped abruptly and her lips turned down, but she didn't try to speak again, as they studied the menu.

Jack looked at me his eyebrows raised slightly. We left the dining room and crossed to the Reception desk.

Caroline looked up, smiling her professional smile. "How can I help?"

"The couple who just went in to lunch," Jack said, "I'm sure I know the guy, he looks very familiar to me."

I swallowed and looked the other way, trying not to laugh.

Caroline glanced right and left, then leaned confidentially over the desk.

"That's Mr. Jankowsky, he's a Hollywood film producer. I think the young lady is going to star in his next production."

Jack nodded his thanks, and we started for the stairs.

"If that girl's going to star in a film, my name's Steven Speilberg," he said.

Back in our room we decided that a snooze would fit the bill. I drew the curtains, took off my shoes and stretched out.

Jack stood by the bed for a few minutes, deep in thought. Then he said, "Why would a Hollywood producer come to an hotel like this? I would have thought the Savoy would be more his scene."

"Unless, of course," I said, "he's not a producer from Hollywood or anywhere else. Suppose, just suppose, that he's here for the diamonds, or maybe the money, or even both?"

"My thoughts exactly," Jack said. He sat on the edge of the bed.

"I think we have to keep an eye on Mr. Jankowsky, and by the way, when I told Caroline that he looked familiar, it was true. I've seen him before. Somewhere. It'll come to me."

With that he lay on the bed, and was out like a light.

"*Dead on Arrival*
"

"*Dead on Arrival*
"

Chapter Seven

Dinner that evening was back up to standard. We felt we were getting our money's worth again. The general atmosphere in the hotel had lightened too, although Robert was still a bit subdued.

We wandered into the bar afterwards, and settled down with a G and T and a malt whisky. I couldn't help but notice that the 'phone man' as I'd christened him, was still absent. His wife and children were well in evidence, however. The two teenagers were haranguing their mother, who looked harassed and uncomfortable.

Presently, the girl jumped up and stormed out, followed shortly after by the boy, whose parting shot was, "So take that and stick it!"

The woman closed her eyes for a moment then nodded to a waiter. A stiff drink soon appeared, after which she gathered up her bag and left.

The couple from the North had obviously enjoyed their meal, as they came into the bar rattling on at the tops of their voices. There was much "Eh upping" and even the occasional "Ba gum."

However, they were a pleasant enough couple, so when they sat down close by we were quite happy to talk to them.

Their names were Arnold and Dolly Barnsworth, and they hailed from Manchester. Apart from our names, we were not required to contribute much after that.

We heard about their son Billy and his wife Natalia (this last vouchsafed with a slight sniff), and their children Giles and Piers. These two names were also followed by a loud sniff, and Arnold's comment of "bloody poncy handles" was shushed by Dolly.

They were just expounding on their daughter Beryl and her husband Dave, when Inspector Collins arrived in the doorway.

He cleared his throat ostentatiously and said, "Pardon me, ladies and gentlemen, I apologise for interrupting your evening, but I must ask you to bear with me."

I felt a groan coming on, while Jack shifted slightly in his chair, and ran his fingers through his hair. That was a sure sign that he felt uneasy.

The Inspector's gaze was focussed upon me, I was sure of it. Oh lordy, don't let him ask me what I was doing poking about outside this morning. I must have been spotted. I knew guilt was writ large on my face.

But he looked at the Barnsworths, then at one or two other people, and I could feel my, by now, sweaty hands beginning to dry.

He cleared his throat again, then said, "As far as I've been given to understand, the deceased gentleman found yesterday evening, was unknown to everyone in the hotel. Nevertheless," he paused and began to look around the room.

"Nevertheless, I think someone in the hotel is aware of his identity," he paused again. "I would like you to think very carefully whether that person is you."

Although he was looking at the ceiling at this point, I was sure that he meant me, or Jack.

No one moved or spoke, even the Barnsworths looked uncomfortable. Then came the sound of a throat being cleared. Not, this time, the Inspector's.

"Could I have a word, Inspector," a pale plump man, aged about fifty or so, sitting tucked away in a corner was waving his fingers.

"Yes sir," Inspector Collins lips twitched in his apology for a smile. "Let's move into the reception hall shall we?"

There was a faint stir and rustle throughout the room, as the two of them left.

"Well, I mean, eh up, what's that about? Eh?" Arnold Barnsworth was all agog.

"Arnie!" Dolly Barnsworth, was flushed and twittering. "It's just like a telly crime play ehn't it? Mrs. Marble or Hercules Poorot!"

Arnie patted her hand. "Now then mother, don't get all unnecessary. All t'same I must say I'm not without some interest."

The more excited they became, the stronger the accents that emerged. They were almost caricatures of the theatrical "North country folk".

Jack and I decided it was time for bed. As politely as we could we bade the Barnsworths "Goodnight".

As we left we heard Arnie calling for "another drop of that there malt, or I'll not sleep the night."

Undressing for bed, something suddenly struck me.

"Jack," I said, "The Barnsworths. Don't you think they're a bit over the top somehow?"

Jack poked his head out of the en-suite, mouth full of toothpaste. "W'ar a ya mean?"

"Well," I said. "Their accents, and the good old North country expressions like 'ba gum' and 'eh up'. It doesn't quite ring true somehow."

He emerged dabbing his face, "You see wrong'uns under every bush you do. Still, now you come to mention it, there was – I don't know – perhaps just.....something."

He climbed into bed, and a few minutes later, I joined him. As we snuggled down together, I reflected on how lucky I was to have Jack. So, I snuggled closer – yes, very lucky.

Chapter Eight

After a good night's sleep, I felt a bit more like my optimistic self.

Jack and I discussed our plan of action over breakfast.

"I think," Jack said, "we should go back to the lane and work our way further afield."

"Yeah," I mumbled, through a mouthful of egg and bacon. "Sounds about right. My waters tell me that maybe the police are concentrating on the hotel grounds a little too intently."

We'd noticed that there was a uniform plodding about the gardens and thickets.

"They could, of course, find something useful," Jack said, "but somehow, I don't think so."

"Unlikely, seeing as we've got a vital piece of evidence," I smirked.

"Don't start getting carried away Pippsy love, remember we have to keep a low profile – at least for now."

So it was that an hour or so later, my husband and I strode purposefully through the gate. This was for the benefit of anyone who might be watching, of course. We hoped that the 'anyone' would assume we were taking a brisk constitutional.

We turned right outside, in the direction of the bushes where we found the diamonds. Then we walked very slowly, eyes proverbially peeled. Unfortunately, the ground was rather dry and cracked, so we couldn't spot any proper footprints.

After about fifteen minutes we were well out of sight of the hotel gate, and hadn't noticed anything out of the ordinary.

"Perhaps we're going about this all wrong," Jack said, after he'd almost ripped his hands to shreds while groping under a particularly hefty bush.

I thought about it.

"Let's find an opening and get into the field on the other side," I said. "It could be that whoever did for the victim was hiding there in wait."

A few yards further on the hedges had thinned considerably. It was comparatively easy to scramble through into a field that seemed to be lying fallow. There must be something planted though, I thought, because there was a scarecrow in the middle, raggedy clothes flapping a little in the breeze.

Out of curiosity I wandered over to have a look. As I got closer, I was surprised at how lifelike the thing appeared.

Talk about Worzel Gummidge, I was thinking, as I stood face to face with it. Then I felt as though I'd been punched in the stomach. It was lifelike all right.

"Jack," I shrieked, "come quickly, come quickly."

Jack had been poking under the bushes, but he sprinted over pretty smartly.

"Oh my Gawd! Oh my good Gawd!" he whispered.

The scarecrow was in fact a body, and a very dead one at that.

Without a word, we turned and carefully made our way back to the gap in the bushes.

Then we ran with all our might back to the hotel. This was something that we couldn't keep from the police - and didn't actually want to anyway.

Inspector Collins had obviously just arrived, as we ran panting and gasping into the hotel reception. He was deep in conversation with two other men, who might also have been police.

"Inspector, please could we talk to you? Nowish?"

He looked over as if about to tell us to wait, but he must have seen our extreme agitation, he said something to the men and marched over.

Before he said anything, I blurted, "We've found a body. In a field about half a mile or so down the lane. You should probably go and have a look."

He looked from me to Jack, who was still gasping. Jack nodded. He couldn't manage any words at this stage.

The Inspector took charge, he called to the other men, "Perkins, Hawkesly, come with me. You too," he said to us. "You'd better show us exactly where you found this body."

There were several guests in the hall by this time, all looking our way. Caroline was craning over the reception desk, eyes starting out of her head. Robert emerged from the office and she gabbled something to him. He turned ashen and dropped like a stone.

Poor Robert, I thought as we trailed in the wake of the Inspector and his men, he really must try and get a hold of himself.

Once we arrived at the field, it was a hive of industry. The Inspector and his men moved with great caution in the direction of Worzel Gummidge. We waited by the hedge. Inspector Collins had been quite definite about that.

"Don't budge from that spot," had been his instructions. But as we had no great desire to look the body in the eye again, that was no problem.

There was much pointing, and easing round the body, then the Inspector pulled out his phone and obviously gave instructions for a medical examiner and scenes of crime officers etc.

He picked his way carefully over to where we waiting, and stood weighing us up for a moment.

"Would you care to tell me, how you came to be in this field?" he said.

"I, that is, we, wanted a brisk walk so we thought we'd just stroll up the lane to see where it led and.....and....." I stopped.

Inspector Collins had raised a sceptical eyebrow.

"Mr. and Mrs. Jack Standage," he said, "Four Eyes Everywhere, I believe that's correct?"

He paused (he was good at pauses, really grabbed the attention). "Did you honestly think we wouldn't have checked up on you? I have been told that you've been quite useful to the police from time to time – I'm not wrong am I?"

"Yes, I mean no, that is you're not wrong," I could hear myself gibbering. So much for all our thinking we were unobserved, incognito, undercover or whatever else.

"You, young lady," his eyes bored into me, "made yourself very much at home with the victim's car. I'm sure you found the suitcases interesting. Or at least the contents of one of them. Your search was quite professional, but you've still got a little way to go." His lips twitched into their smile.

"And Mr. Standage, that's a nice little gadget that you've got. I'd like to look it over some time, when we're not so busy." His lips twitched again.

We stood like two naughty children receiving a dressing down. I wondered if we were in trouble, real trouble that is. He hadn't mentioned diamonds or notebooks so far, but I thought it was only a matter of time.

"There is one other small matter." He had turned away, then swung back suddenly – like the pauses, a very effective manoeuvre.

This is it, I thought. He's never going to believe that we're just looking after them.

"I would appreciate it, if you could keep me informed of any other developments that might come to your attention." With a wave of his hand we were dismissed.

We tottered back down the lane to the hotel. "I thought he'd got us bang to rights about the diamonds," I said.

Jack nodded glumly.

"Now what are we going to do?" he said. "If I'd only listened to you, we could have been shot of the bloody things. Instead of which, we're going to have to find some way of leaving them for someone else to find."

Chapter Nine

Jack and I mulled over our situation while enjoying a cup of coffee. That's to say, the coffee was a lifeline, strong and black, to clear our heads.

"We could just shove the bag back where we found it," I suggested.

Jack thought for a moment.

"I'm not struck on that," he said. "Somebody's obviously going to be looking for the diamonds, and if we've hidden them it could be tricky. Think about it Pippsy, Collins sussed us out fairly smartly, so it's possible that someone with a lot to gain and much to hide could do the same."

This certainly hit home. I didn't fancy being buttonholed by someone who'd killed once, possibly twice, or maybe even more!

"Well, shall we just go and make a clean breast of it?" I said. "Give him the loot and the notebook and say something like, 'we were just looking after them'?"

Even to my ears this sounded thin, and Jack snorted with derision.

"We'd be clapped into cuffs for tampering with evidence straight off," he said.

I had to agree, he was probably right.

We sat in silence for a few moments then I had a brainwave. "That guy earlier on, you know the little pale bloke, who was waving to Collins, why don't we find out what he knows."

Jack snorted again, "What earthly use do you think he'll be?"

"He must know something," I said stubbornly, "or why would he have wanted to talk to Collins, who surely suspected someone of knowing something?"

My other half sat silent again. Then he said, "Alright, we'll try. But bear in mind he might not want to talk to us."

Half an hour later, we had pinned down Joshua Carmichael, as he turned out to be, and although he seemed a little nervous he agreed to talk to us.

We introduced ourselves and our agency. This seemed to alarm him, as he turned paler than ever, and began fiddling with his tie.

"There's no need to worry Mr. Carmichael," Jack assured him, "we're not going to cause any trouble. We just need to ask you a few questions."

He continued to fiddle with his tie.

"So," Jack began, "did you know the victim in the car? When the Inspector asked us who knew him, you put your hand up so to speak."

"I didn't exactly know him," Carmichael said, "but I was tasked with meeting him in, what we term, a business connection."

"So," Jack said again, "he was a business acquaintance then?"

"Well, not an acquaintance, no. I was acting for another party, who was looking to have certain items they had acquired, valued with a view to selling them. It was my business to value the said items, and then arrange payment if there was a mutually amicable agreement."

Jack pulled his lower lip between his thumb and forefinger, looking steadily at Carmichael.

"In other words Mr. Carmichael, you were fencing them," Jack said.

The little man turned if possible, even paler. "No, no, no Mr. Standage. I have an impeccable reputation, I was merely acting as a go-between, as the two parties concerned could not be seen ..... that is, it was inconvenient for them to meet. It's proving very difficult all round, firstly the sudden demise of one party, then the disappearance of the items."

He pulled out his handkerchief, and dabbed his forehead. He was sweating profusely.

"Could these so called 'items' be diamonds by any chance?" Jack asked.

I thought Carmichael was going to have a heart attack. He gasped, mouth opening and closing uselessly.

"How could you possibly know that, Mr. Standage?" he mumbled at last.

"The items are missing. I was to have taken delivery of them two days ago, except that no one arrived. Then that poor man turned up dead, and when I tried to phone the other party on the number I had been given, it just rang and rang. I tried a dozen times without any success. I'm in a difficult position. I don't know what my next move should be."

I began to feel sorry for the little man, his distress was so great. Should we hand the diamonds over to him? Should we tell him we knew where they were? It was a dilemma of massive proportions.

We sat looking at him, as he mopped his face and fiddled with his tie.

At last I said, "Look Mr. Carmichael, you obviously have a name for the dead man, so can you tell us, was he known to the police?"

"Oh, my goodness, yes. I had no idea of course, that there was anything suspicious. I'm a business man, my integrity is everything. I couldn't believe my ears when the police told me, that is, said Mr. Pu........ I mean Smith, had something of a reputation."

Jack pursed his lips, and I looked down at my hands. I wished we had a tenner for every time we've heard a response like that one.

"Well, Mr. Carmichael, you've helped us a lot. Be assured if we learn anything of value we shan't keep it to ourselves," Jack smiled.

Carmichael bared his teeth in what I supposed, passed for a smile. We all stood up, and went our separate ways.

Over lunch we discussed the conversation with Carmichael.

"We know he's obviously up the creek without a paddle," Jack said. "Whoever popped Mr. 'I mean Smith' is going to finger him first. It won't be any use him saying the messenger didn't arrive, he's going to be head of the queue, and if he lets on that we were asking questions, we're going to be next."

"There's nothing for it," I said, "we've got to tell Inspector Collins the truth, and throw ourselves on his mercy. I for one, don't fancy standing in the middle of a field scaring the birds for the next few years."

We hadn't enjoyed our lunch. There was nothing wrong with the food, only with us.

Reluctantly, Jack agreed that owning up was the best solution. The Inspector as it happened was seated at a table, drinking coffee and eating sandwiches, while perusing a sheaf of papers.

We made our way tentatively to his table, where we stood nervously trying to think how to begin. He looked up.

"Ah, Mr. and Mrs. Standage again. What can I do for you, or perhaps, what can you do for me?"

"We've got a small confession to make," I said, between dry lips. "I'm afraid we haven't told you everything. We meant to, but we really didn't know how to explain."

I ran out of words, and just stood there.

The Inspector dabbed his lips with his napkin.

"Delicious sandwiches," he said, "just hit the spot. Now then, have you come to tell me about the diamonds?"

"Dead on Arrival
"

"Dead on Arrival
"

Chapter Ten

If the Inspector had reached out and slapped my face, I couldn't have been more shocked. I risked a glance at Jack. His mouth was open, as if awaiting a dental examination.

After a minute we were waved to a couple of chairs.

He settled back and said, "Now then, tell me the full story."

Jack cleared his throat. "I'll begin shall I?"

At receiving a nod, he launched into the saga, starting with the discovery of the body by Robert, and ending with our conversation with Joshua Carmichael.

The Inspector who had not spoken, broke his silence.

"Ah, Mr. Carmichael, I wondered if you would have engaged him in discussion."

"We thought that he might've given us some clue as to what was going on," I said, "but he seemed more concerned with assuring us of his complete integrity. I have to say, we were not that convinced."

Surprisingly, the Inspector said, "Mr. Carmichael is not altogether unknown to us. He has been involved in similar negotiations before. We have unfortunately, never been in a position to discover exactly what his role was in those negotiations, other than, as he puts it "a go-between". In addition, on this occasion, he neglected to mention both the money and the diamonds."

Jack chipped in, "Just what did he tell you Inspector?"

"Merely that he had arranged to meet the deceased, to deliver certain items of value, which in turn had been delivered to him. He was at pains to assure me that he knew neither the deceased nor the messenger."

Jack tapped his teeth with a fingernail.

"Is it possible, Inspector, that the poor unfortunate guarding the field up the road was the messenger?"

"Mr. Standage your acuity does you credit. That gentleman too, was known to us. A small timer, who, shall we say ran errands for the upper echelons of the criminal fraternity. It appears that on this occasion, something went awry. The man was quite badly beaten before being hung up. The cause of death is still being investigated, but it's likely that he died from his injuries."

Jack and I sat very still. I pictured the dying man tied to the supporting pole, and if he was conscious, just hanging there waiting for....... ugh, it didn't bear thinking about.

"I think it would be in your own best interests, to pass the diamonds to me," the Inspector said. "Whoever killed these two men is obviously very keen to get their hands on them. If there should be even a suggestion that you are in possession it could be – well, need I go any further?"

I could feel my face draining of blood. The Inspector leaned over and patted my hand.

"I'm sure you will be perfectly safe, my dear young lady, once the diamonds are in the hands of the police."

Jack and I nodded vigorously.

"I'll nip and get them now, shall I?" I asked.

"That might be advisable," the Inspector's lips twitched into their smile. "Then you can forget all of this ever happened, and continue with your holiday."

There was nothing that appealed to me more. I left the dining room with almost indecent haste, leaving Jack with the Inspector.

Back in our room, I retrieved the little suede bag from the wardrobe. After thinking about it, I decided that the notebook should be passed on too. I flipped it open and studied it once again.

Something struck me. Page after page of days, times and numbers. I stood holding the notebook, and wondering. It must be a code of some kind. I was loath to pass it over without giving it another go.

The mystery was deepening by the minute. Oh well, I thought, Inspector Collins would undoubtedly have experts for unravelling codes. I was surprised that he hadn't mentioned the notebook. If the police had searched the suitcases why hadn't they given the book to the Inspector? Odd, very odd – something wasn't quite right somewhere.

I tucked the notebook into my handbag. No need to volunteer anything, just wait and see if he mentions it.

I thought I'd better get downstairs, before he became suspicious. Still, as I went back to the dining room, I felt - I don't know, uncomfortable. A kind of itch that I couldn't quite reach.

Jack and the Inspector were getting along famously. I approached the table without their noticing me, and I heard

Collins say, "So in the end we just had to let him go, although we knew he was guilty. The case is in the dead file."

I wondered what that was all about. It seemed a strange conversation. Not one you would expect a Detective Inspector to be having with a member of the public. Even if that member was a private eye.

They turned as I came to the table, the Inspector twitching his smile again.

"Well, well, my dear Mrs. Standage, I trust you found everything in order?"

"Yes, yes," I said, opening my bag. I took out the little bag and passed it over. Jack looked as though he'd had a sudden recollection.

"By the way, Inspector," he began, "Pippsy also found......"

"A lot of dirty laundry," I whipped in, giving Jack a hard stare. He looked puzzled, but didn't pursue what I was sure he'd been going to say.

The Inspector had opened the neck of the bag and was peering in. He appeared unaware that anything was amiss, in fact he seemed not to have registered what passed between us.

"That all seems quite in order," he said. "Of course, I shan't know for sure, until the stones have been examined, and we've had a further talk with Mr. Carmichael."

He stood up. "That concludes our business I think. You've been most helpful, even if you did get off to a rocky start. I hope that your agency continues to flourish. You seem a very competent young couple, and who knows, we may have need to call on you sometime."

He twitched, and strode out.

I stood looking after him.

"What were you two talking about, while I was getting the stones?" I asked.

Jack pursed his lips. "Well," he said, "I must say it was a bit strange, he told me about several unsolved cases. All involving gemstones, if I remember correctly. By the way, why did you stop me from telling him about the notebook, and why didn't you give it to him?"

"I don't know," I said. "But I felt that something wasn't quite kosher. Couldn't put a finger on it – just something."

Jack shrugged. "Well at least we're out of it now."

"Don't be too sure," I told him. "That notebook's some sort of code. I think we should try and crack it."

Jack gave a groan.

"Oh no, here we go again," he said.

“Dead on Arrival
”

“Dead on Arrival
”

Chapter Eleven

We spent a large portion of the afternoon strolling around the grounds. I kept an eye on the uniform who had acquired a companion. They were still peering and prodding in the undergrowth.

"I wonder what the boys in blue are looking for?" I mused to Jack. "After all, we've given over the diamonds, and I presume the suitcases have been removed from the boot. Funny though, they haven't towed the car away for examination. We know from previous experiences that once a bod 's been carted off they tear the surroundings apart."

Jack mulled it over for a while. I got quite concerned. He was pulling on his lower lip so hard, I feared he'd finish up like one of those African plate-lipped men and women.

The picture this conjured up made me laugh out loud, much to Jack's surprise. When I explained, he chuckled then shook his head.

"Perhaps they're looking for the notebook," he said at last. "I'm sure Collins must be wondering where it is – that is, if he knows it exists."

We decided to go back to our room, and have another bash at deciphering the code – if indeed it was a code.

As we passed through the reception hall, Mr. Jankowsky appeared, his mobile phone clamped to his ear. He was talking rapidly in a low voice, his beady little eyes darting this way and that all the time.

"Obviously closing some big deal," I murmured to Jack.

As we passed him, I could have sworn I heard the word 'diamonds' followed by 'missing'. Then, I could have been wrong, so much was milling about in my brain. Jack didn't seem to have noticed, so I thought I was probably overreacting.

Once in our room we pulled off our shoes, propped the pillows up on the bed and settled down. A pad, pencils, a pocket dictionary (one should never be without one), and the all important notebook.

We began by noting down some of the days. Then taking the alphabetic number of each letter and trying to link it to the times.

I raked out my calculator, and we variously added, multiplied, subtracted and divided.

Not a sausage.

My head began to throb.

"It's no use," I said, "if it's a code, we're not going to break it this way." Jack nodded, looking gloomy.

"Still," he said, "it must mean something. I guess we're just not on the right wavelength."

It was my turn to nod gloomily.

It was getting near to dinner time, so I put the book back in my bag, and made for the shower.

"We'll have to give it a rest then try again later," I said.

Jack switched on the T.V. The early evening news was just beginning.

I had barely finished, when Jack yelled to me. I scampered into the bedroom, still wrapped in my towel.

The newsreader, looking grave, was talking about a missing businessman. The man in question had disappeared two days ago. He'd left home, en route for a meeting, but had not been heard from since. His wife claimed that he always rang her on his arrival, and she'd had no idea where he was going.

Jack and I looked at each other. Odd. It became even odder, when it transpired that the wife's name was Sandra, wife of Harry Purvis.

"Pu.....I mean Smith," we said.

Why hadn't the police told the poor woman, that the man found outside our hotel was almost certainly her husband.

"I'm beginning to become very suspicious of Inspector Collins," I said.

Jack agreed.

"Let's ring the local constabulary, and speak to him," I suggested. "If he's there, we can ask him why there's a report out that Purvis is missing?"

After hunting high and low for a telephone directory, we rang reception and asked Caroline to connect us to the local police. She was a little taken aback, to say the least.

After a few minutes a slow measured voice assured us that we were speaking to the police.

"Could I speak to Detective Inspector Collins?" I asked.

There was a long pause then the voice said, "There is no officer of that name attached to this station".

"Are you sure?" I squeaked.

"Madam, there are only three members of the service here. I would be certain of their names wouldn't I?"

Jack seized the handset. "To whom am I speaking," he asked in his most authoritative voice.

"Sergeant Jones," I heard.

"Well, Sergeant Jones," Jack went on, "two days ago, a man was found dead in a car in the grounds of The Flowerdew Hotel, where we are presently residing. The police were called, and an Inspector Collins arrived on the premises to investigate. He returned several times, and appeared to have the case in hand. Now, who is he?"

There was complete and utter silence at the other end. Jack and I waited, then Jack said, "Hello, are you still there, or have you gone for a cup of tea?"

There came a kind of splutter then Sergeant Jones said, in a less than confident tone, "Yes, I'm still here, but I can't understand what you mean. About bodies, and Inspectors having cases in hand. We know absolutely nothing about it here. I think this is a hoax call, I must tell you that there are serious penalties for making calls of this kind........"

Jack cut him off. "This is no hoax," he said quietly (quiet often does it). "You may visit the hotel and question everyone here, who will confirm what I have told you."

Silence again. Then the Sergeant said, "I shall do that, sir. Could I have your name?"

After Jack put the phone down, and I'd finished my interrupted toilette, we sat on the edge of the bed holding hands tightly.

"I'm liking all of this less and less," I said, trying to control the quaver in my voice.

Jack squeezed my hand. "There's probably a logical explanation babe. Collins maybe comes from another district and somehow intercepted the call made from......."

I looked at him. He was pulling at that lip again.

"Can you remember who called the police? It wasn't Caroline, was it?"

I sat and thought, picturing the chaos that had ensued after the body was discovered.

"No, it wasn't Caroline – someone else, a guest, said they'd done it."

"Can you think who?"

But I couldn't – all I could see was the staff and guests milling around, while Robert played the Dying Swan.

"It was a man, I'm pretty sure of that," Jack said.

"What makes you think so?"

"Just a vague recollection of someone saying that they'd rung the police." That lip will be down to his navel soon, I thought.

He sighed and gave up.

"Let's get some dinner, before we have to start answering questions again."

As we went downstairs, I kept thinking about the entries in the notebook. Suppose, just suppose that they were what they seemed. Days and times. I kept quiet. Jack was still thinking deeply, but I fancied that he was getting hungry for his dinner. My husband is a great lover of food!

We were surprised to see that the dining room was well supported tonight. Usually there's comings and goings at meal times, but for some reason everyone was in within ten minutes of each other.

We surreptitiously checked out the other guests.

The Barnsworths, in full flow of course.

Carmichael, looking as though he was trying to disappear into his corner.

Mr. Jankowsky, with his blonde companion, who looked and sounded a little more restrained tonight.

Then there was the family of four. The husband was seated with them, but didn't appear to be enjoying the experience.

A young couple whom I'd not noticed before, were sitting holding hands across the table. Probably honeymooners, I thought. All the drama of the last two days must have taken the edge off it.

There were a couple of men on their own, probably enjoying business expense accounts.

Finally, the foursome in their designer suits and dresses.

I tried not to be too obvious, but I couldn't help watching them. Somehow, they didn't quite fit at an hotel like The Flowerdew. And, what did they do in the evenings, or during the day for that matter? The surrounding area was hardly bursting with nightlife, or designer shops.

Then it hit me. One of the men was the guest who had claimed to have rung the police.

I leant over to Jack, who was just scraping up the last of his chocolate pot dessert. (How does he keep so trim, considering the type of food he enjoys? I only have to look at a cream cake, and I'm four pounds heavier!).

"Hon, the four by the window. The guy in the pale grey suit, the blonde one, I think he's the man who said he'd rung the police."

Jack dabbed his lips, and leaned back in his chair nonchalantly angling so that he could look at the man in question.

"You sure?" he asked.

I nodded, "Yes, pretty much. I'm sure it's the blonde hair. Must have registered more than I thought."

As we stood up to leave, Caroline came in accompanied by a quite personable man, aged around thirty. Sergeant Jones, I thought. Which proved to be the case.

We strolled towards the lounge, making small talk with the Sergeant, who was suprisingly adept at it. I glanced over to the window. The four people seated there, while not exactly looking anxious, had a slight shiftiness about them.

The man in the grey suit was leaning forward and talking rapidly. The other three were in various stages of unease. Or so it seemed to me.

By the time we reached the lounge, I'd made up my mind that there was something decidedly dodgy about those four people. We sat down and Jack called the waiter.

"I'm sure you would like a drink?" he said to the sergeant.

"Well, that's very civil of you Mr. Standage," he said. "If you wouldn't mind, a snifter of brandy would be very welcome."

When we were settled with our drinks Sergeant Jones opened the batting.

"Now, could you tell me everything you know, or can think of, with regard to this Inspector Collins."

Going turn and turn about, Jack and I gave an account of everything which had happened during the last couple of days.

Sergeant Jones listened intently, only interrupting if he became confused (his word) by the wealth of detail we imparted.

When we had finally finished, he sat quietly for several minutes.

"I think," he said at last, "we had better telephone my superiors in Cheltenham."

Did I say that the hotel was situated in the Cotswolds?

He went on, "After our telephone conversation, I searched our lists of officers in this area, and I couldn't find a trace of an Inspector Collins."

Somehow, this didn't surprise me. I was sure it didn't surprise Jack either.

"Well," I said, "the car is still on the drive, even if it is empty. But we think it belongs to that missing businessman Harry Purvis. Mr. Carmichael may be able to confirm that."

The sergeant nodded.

"Yes, indeed, Mr. Carmichael is a featured player in all this, isn't he?"

I was warming to Sergeant Jones by the minute. He was as unlike a 'country bobby' as could possibly be imagined. Even Jack was impressed, I could tell.

"What could have happened to the bodies?" I asked. "I mean, you don't just pop someone into your car and do a bit of fly tipping do you?"

"I think," the Sergeant said slowly, "that it points to a very sophisticated organisation, entailing God knows what, but probably involving considerable sums of money and precious stones."

"And a spot of murder too, by the looks of it," Jack said.

Sergeant Jones gave a wry nod.

"Couldn't have put it better myself, Mr. Standage."

"What should we do in the meantime? Until you've heard from your superiors?" I asked.

"Keep a low profile, Mrs. Standage. It looks as though, whatever all this is about, could be dangerous. We don't want to be searching for more bodies, do we?"

I shook my head vigorously, and Jack ran his hand through his hair.

Sergeant Jones stood up, holding out his hand, which we were happy to shake.

"You've been more than co-operative," he said. "I'm sure that whoever takes over this case will be very grateful. By the way," he pursed his lips, and half smiled. "I took the liberty of running a quick check on you. 'Four Eyes Everywhere', am I correct?"

We nodded.

"According to my information, you've sailed a bit close to the wind on one or two occasions. You seem to have had some lucky escapes, but I think you may have moved into a different league this time." With that parting shot he took his leave.

Jack and I sat down again, and ordered another round.

"That foursome by the window," I began.

"Don't go there. Don't even think it," Jack said firmly. "I mean it Pippsy. You heard what the sergeant said. I don't want you disappearing all of a sudden then turning up as a corpse."

I beamed at him. "Would you miss me then," I almost simpered.

"Yes," he said. "Who would answer the phones and make the tea, if you weren't around?"

Chapter Twelve

I tossed and turned all night. Jack however, slept like a baby. I could have killed him. Why wasn't he tossing and turning? We had worries, and worries are for worrying about.

Sergeant Jones's warnings came back again and again. "A different league," he'd said. "Sailed close to the wind," he'd said. Perhaps we had been lucky in the past, although I believe you make your own luck. Never mind, I'd better keep that 'low profile' he mentioned.

All the same, I thought, it would be nice just to keep half an eye on the foursome. Surely I could talk Jack round. I usually could.

I managed to nod off, just as it was getting light, and the birds had broken into the 'Hallelujah Chorus'.

I woke about half past eight and groaned. My eyes felt like lumps of hot coal in a furnace, and I ached everywhere.

Jack was doing his Pavarotti impersonation in the shower.

I groaned again, and dived underneath the bedclothes, hands over my ears. It's not that Jack's got a bad voice...... just not what I wanted to hear at that moment.

He bounded into the bedroom calling, "Good morning, moon of my delight. It's a lovely day. What say we drive into Cheltenham for a spot of retail therapy?"

Now normally that would have had me up dancing the rumba, but not today. Not after the night I'd had. Besides which, I'd got to try to 'silver tongue' him into taking a closer look at the foursome.

I sat up slowly, and spoke even more so.

"I think I would like to stay close to the hotel today hon, if you don't mind that is?"

Jack looked as though he couldn't believe his ears. Pippsy turning her back on a shopping trip, no it wasn't possible.

"Are you feeling iffy, pet?" he asked. "I must say, you do look a bit pasty. Yes, if that's what you want we'll just have a little walk in the gardens, and do a spot of reading. Do Cheltenham when you feel more like it?"

I smiled wanly. Hurdle one, safely crossed.

I'll begin the plan of campaign after breakfast, I thought. All at once I began to feel a whole lot better.

The foursome was not at breakfast. At least not when we were there. I wondered if they had risen early.

Jack tucked into a hearty plateful of egg and bacon, followed by toast and marmalade. But for the life of me, I couldn't fancy anything more than a bowl of cornflakes.

To be honest, I was in a sweat trying to come up with some story which would enable us – that is me – to find out more about the foursome.

However, I was in luck. Just as we were leaving the dining room, the blonde man and his wife? Partner? Or whatever, were coming downstairs.

"You go on up," I told Jack. "I'm going to have a quick word with Caroline. Find out how Robert is this morning." Well, it was the only excuse I could think of on the spur of the moment.

I lingered by the reception desk, pretending to look at the various brochures and leaflets on display.

"Let's nip over to Broadway," I heard the woman say, "there's a good leather shop there, I really need a jacket.

Broadway! Leather Jacket! Didn't sound much like the conversation of internationl criminals.

The blonde guy was shaking his head, so I lingered a bit longer.

"Mags, we must get our business sorted out. That's one reason we came," I heard.

Now, I thought, that's a bit more like it. He went on talking earnestly.

"We'll make all the arrangements this end. Once we get the dates for delivering the merchandise, we can take a bit of time off for leather jackets, or whatever you like."

That's it I said to myself, he's thinking Diamonds, with a capital D.

We'd got to follow them. I looked around a bit helplessly for a minute then I called Caroline.

"I've got to pop out for half an hour – need some moisture cream, the stuff in the bathroom doesn't suit my skin. Could you give my husband a bell. Tell him I won't be long, just need a Boots."

She looked a bit surprised, but agreed to ring Jack.

I flew down the outside steps and made for the car park. I could see the couple getting into their car, latest model current number plate – just what you would expect.

Luckily, I always have a spare set of keys in my bag. Trying to look inconspicuous, I watched the couple drive to the gate.

As quickly as I dared, I followed. At the gate I saw them disappearing down the lane to my left, at a fair old rate. I took a deep breath and dropped in behind them.

The roads around the hotel were very rural, which made for difficulty in following another car. But, I kept at it, and when a major junction was indicated, I was glad to see their car just ahead.

Getting onto a straight stretch, I sighed with relief, just making sure I didn't get too close. I have of course been engaged in following vehicles in the past, so I'm not a complete novice.

Eventually, they turned left at a sign for Bourton-on-the-Water. Having been there once or twice, I couldn't picture it as a hotbed of criminal activity – but what did I know?

We bowled through this picture postcard setting, and continued along for a further mile or two. A few idiots, who should have been arrested, attempted to overtake, but I was having none of it. I'd come this far, there was no way I was going to lose them now.

At last they turned into the driveway of a large property. I pulled in to the side, as close as I could without being too obvious.

Trying to appear casual, in case anyone was watching, I strolled through the entrance, and promptly dived into the bushes, happily for me positioned to both left and right.

The car was parked outside an imposing frontage. I could see the couple standing on the steps leading to the front door, presumably waiting to be admitted.

After a minute or so, I saw the front door open, and a stout, motherly looking woman (probably the housekeeper, it looked that sort of house), obviously asking them their business.

It was sickening that I was just too far away to hear what was said. I could have done with Jack's little gizmo.

Whatever they said, it was enough for them to be ushered inside.

Blow, bother and words of that ilk, I said to myself. I'll just have to get a bit closer, and hope that they're in a room with an open window. Trying to keep below window height, I made a quick dash across the drive, and huddled under a front window.

My luck held, the window was open, and I could hear the murmur of voices.

"We've got fifty ......" (too indistinct), " that's what you wanted wasn't it? We can deliver in about a week, if that's alright?"

There was a mumble in response, presumably the owner of the house. This was followed by some remark from the woman, and a burst of laughter.

I dared to peep over the window cill. Fortunately the three occupants had their backs to the window. I could see however, that it was a very amicable meeting. The blonde man had his hand on the shoulder of a second man, who was holding the woman's hand and nodding his head.

"It's very good of you to break into your holiday like this," the second man said.

"No problem, no problem," this was the blonde man. "Mags wants a trip to Broadway for a leather jacket, can't think what on earth she needs with another coat – but that's the ladies for you."

The laughter broke out again. If I'd been Mags, I would have socked them both on jaw for a comment like that.

They began making their way to the door, so I beat a speedy retreat. I was back in the bushes as the front door opened.

"So we're all set then, fifty cases of our best yogurts, in mixed flavours. Be with you, by the end of next week. Nice doing business with you, I'll get a hard copy of the contract in the post in a day or so. Cheers mate."

I've never felt such a fool in my life – well maybe once or twice – but this beat everything. Yogurts in mixed flavours. Jack was right I do go off at half cock, which reminded me, what was I going to tell him? He'd have a fit first then tell me it served me right. Which of course, it did.

I waited until the couple had driven off, and got back to the car as quickly as I could.

Heading back to The Flowerdew, I tried to think of some plausible reason for my sudden disappearance. I totally forgot I was supposed to be visiting Boots for moisture lotion.

Back at the hotel, I found Jack sitting in the lounge reading the daily paper. He was fit to be tied when I began a garbled tale. I should have known I couldn't fool him.

"Stop making up such drivel," he said. "I knew you were up to something, the minute Caroline told me you'd careered off for face cream or some such. All that flannel about wanting to stay close to the hotel. I couldn't believe it. You've been chasing off after some fancied suspects or other haven't you?"

I had to admit it. Finally I told him the whole stupid story. I had to admit my conviction that the blonde man had made the call to the police, was totally wrong.

At the words yogurts in mixed flavours, I thought he was going to rupture himself. He nearly fell of his chair laughing. In fact, Caroline came out of the back office to see what was happening.

"It's nothing," I said sheepishly, "he's just heard a story he finds amusing."

Chapter Thirteen

For the remainder of the day I had to steel myself. Jack's idea of humour can be very infantile. For example, he asked me if I'd like yogurt for lunch, then suggested that maybe I would like to visit Broadway to buy a jacket. All this accompanied by guffaws of laughter.

I adore my husband, but his sense of humour gets up my nose sometimes.

It occurred to me that I really should forget about crime and criminals, and just enjoy our holiday. After all, the police were paid to solve crimes, and we had at least pointed them in the right direction – more or less.

So, next morning when Jack suggested the trip to Cheltenham again, I agreed with alacrity. Of course he couldn't resist a little dig, and said we could look for a nice leather jacket.

I kicked him, hard. It shut him up temporarily, but he still kept looking sideways at me and smirking. That and the occasional reference to Miss Marple or Kinsey Milhone – what a plonker!

We had a pleasant drive to Cheltenham, taking our time and admiring the beautiful scenery. Neither of us felt particularly hungry, so we made do with a cup of coffee in a pleasant little cafe.

Feeling relaxed we strolled along the main shopping parade, stopping now and then to admire some particularly attractive item. I'd put all thoughts of diamonds and murders and notebooks out of my head, so it was a total shock when I saw Inspector Collins leave a jeweller's and cross the road to a car.

Jack must have noticed because he said, "Pippsy, are you alright? You look struck all of a heap."

"Look, look," I managed to gasp. "It's Collins, over there, just got into that black Vauxhall."

Jack looked, but it was too late, Collins had pulled out and driven off at some speed.

"Oh Pippsy, you must have imagined it. What would Collins be doing in Cheltenham, he's got everything he wanted. It was just someone who resembled him I'm sure."

I shook my head, "No, it was Collins, I'm positive. He came out of that jeweller's, I'm going in there to see what I can find out, you can come or not, as you like. But I know what I saw."

With that, I took off. Jack, taken by surprise, had to sprint to catch me.

"Pippsy," he protested, as we opened the shop door, "what on earth are you going to say?"

"I'll think of something, don't you worry," I told him.

The shop had no customers, but the proprietor or manager or whatever he was, hovered behind his counter, smiling (hopefully, I expect).

"We're interested in diamonds," I said. It was the first thing that came into my head.

"Ah, diamonds, yes," he was almost rubbing his hands. "What had madam, sir, in mind? A ring? A brooch? Perhaps a nice pair of earrings, we have some very unusual contemporary designs, just right for the younger, more stylish lady."

Smarmy b......, I thought. I smiled back at him. I could feel Jack shifting from one foot to the other. Oh well, the guy probably thinks Jack's uneasy about the amount he'll be expected to fork out.

"We were told that your establishment has diamonds which can be put into settings of the customer's choice?" A bit chancy perhaps, but nothing ventured etc.

Jack gave a huge cough, then seized his handkerchief and pretended to blow his nose. His anxiety was almost palpable.

"Really, madam, may I ask who recommended us?" The smile had become a little wary. Perhaps I was on the right track. Mustn't overdo it though.

"I don't actually recall, who it was," I said as ingenuously as I could. "We have several acquaintances who are interested in diamonds."

Jack's cough worsened.

"Perhaps you would care to furnish me with their names?"

I put on a thoughtful expression, furrowing my brow and tapping my chin with my forefinger.

"I think one of them could have been Mr. Carmichael. Then there was Mr. Collins, of course, and Mr. Jankowsky." I was really getting into the swing now. I paused meaningfully.

"I'm afraid, none of those names means anything to me," he said quickly. Rather too quickly I thought, so I gave him the sort of hard stare that would have rivalled Paddington's.

"Well, the name Carmichael does ring a bell, but I'm not sure if remember the gentleman too clearly."

At last, an admission of sorts. We stood looking at each other.

"Try me," I said.

"A smallish gentleman, as I recall. Like myself, in the trade. Did valuations and acted as an intermediary from time to time."

"That sounds like him," I said. I dug a little further.

"So, the name Collins means nothing to you?"

This time the man's face cleared. "Nothing whatsoever," he said positively.

Obviously the bogus inspector was using another name. I decided to plunge in.

"As we were about to enter, we noticed a man leaving here whom we recognised. Unfortunately he drove off before we could speak to him. Can't just bring his name to mind, I'm sure I'll think of it in a minute." I furrowed the brow again. By this time, Jack had subsided into a chair positioned at the counter, put there no doubt, for men whose ladies were about to cost them a small fortune.

"Ah, Mr. Fitzgerald," was the response, while I nodded, smiled and said, "Yes, of course, silly me, my mind's a sieve sometimes."

"Yes, Mr. Fitzgerald," he went on, "a very knowledgeable customer."

I bet he is, I thought.

"I'm not, naturally, able to disclose why he was visiting us, that would be indiscreet. Suffice it to say, our proposed transaction may be of interest to you in the future, if you're still looking for stones that could be set in a style of your choice that is."

I understood him to be suggesting that some diamonds were now in his possession. Jack who had been slumped forward, suddenly sat up straight.

"Do you have, by any chance," he said, "a phone number for old Fitzgerald? We lost contact with him, and can't find his new number."

I could have hugged him, that touch about 'old Fitzgerald' was perfect.

"I do, I do," was the reply, "but I don't think I should just hand it out to anyone."

"We're not just anyone," I said, fluttering my eyelashes and coming over all girlish. I even tried the odd wiggle.

"Of course not, dear, dear, I didn't mean to imply......" the poor man twittered, turning pink. "But Mr. Fitzgerald is an extremely important man, and I have to be very careful........I mean I can't just....." He stopped, looking distraught.

"Mr.?" Jack paused looking questioningly.

"Polstetter," was the reply.

"Yes, well Mr. Polstetter," Jack continued, "suppose you had written old Fitz's number down and happened to leave it on the counter, and we happened to see it – it couldn't do any harm, could it?"

Polstetter, wrung his hands and looked right and left. Then he opened a drawer, took out a sheet of paper and casually (or as casually as he could) dropped it on the counter.

There was both a mobile number, and a landline. We both looked, I memorised the mobile and Jack the landline. We have this manoevre down to a fine art now, having needed it many times in the past.

"I haven't seen you," he muttered, "and I think that it would be better – although I hate to turn away business – if I didn't see you again."

"It's been a pleasure to talk to you Mr. Polstetter," I told him, "and you may be sure that we shall recommend your establishment to all our friends."

We endeavoured not to look too hasty as we left, but neither of us could wait to follow this lead.

Once outside, we raced for the car. Safe inside, we scribbled down the memorised numbers, then began to plan.

"The landline might be the best bet," I said. "I could pretend to be doing market research or something, and angle for his address."

"That's no good," Jack said firmly. "If he's anything like us, he'll give short shrift to market researchers. No, we'll have to be more subtle than that."

"We could disguise our voices, and threaten to blackmail him with our knowledge?" I suggested.

Jack pondered, pulling his lip – by the end of this little caper that lip will be twice its proper size, I thought.

"No," he said finally, "we could find ourselves in dire straits and then some, if he latches on to us. Remember, two bodies have turned up already. Now I'm not saying that he's responsible, but I think we should keep an open mind about that."

Dammit, I thought, why is he always so logical? Gets on my wick sometimes. We sat there for half an hour, suggesting this or that idea and discarding them one by one.

Suddenly, I had an idea. "Got it," I squeaked. "Got it, got it, got it!"

"We ring up and say we're from Polstetter's, his secretary or a repairer or his boss, or I don't know, something of that sort, and then tell him there's a problem, and we need him back at the shop at once. What d'you think?"

"It could work," Jack said thoughtfully. "But when he turns up, if he turns up, what then? Do we leap out and face him? No, we hang around and see what happens. Of course Polstetter is going to tell him he didn't make any phone call, so Collins or Fitzgerald or whatever he's called, is going to be suspicious. He might think that his house or office, whatever, is under threat, so chances are he'll head straight there, and we follow him. Yes?"

"Jack, you're wonderful," I plonked a kiss on him.

"Now we'll have to be careful when we make the call. Can you do one of your voices?" Jack asked.

"Whatever you like, Welsh, Irish, Sloane Ranger, a touch of Essex perhaps?" I was loving this.

"Just take it easy, don't overdo it. Don't give him too much info. Simply say that your boss Mr. Polstetter would like him to come over as quickly as poss. because there's a problem. And if he asks, no, you don't know what it is."

As Jack keyed in the number on his mobile, I thought what a let down if Collins isn't there.

The phone rang a few times, and I was waiting for an answer message to cut in, but the receiver was picked up. A woman's voice said, "Hello, Fitzgerald residence."

I was a bit taken aback, as it was not quite what I was expecting. I cleared my throat and said brightly with a touch of Irish blarney, "Could I speak to Mr. Fitzgerald if you please?"

The woman said, "Hold on," then called "Fitz, phone for you. Some Irish woman by the sound of it." This last was an aside.

After a few minutes we heard, "This is Fitzgerald. Who's this?"

"I'm Miss Reilly, Mr. Polstetter's assistant. Mr. Polstetter wonders if you could come to the store imminently, there's a small problem."

"What sort of problem, and why does he need me?" Collins/Fitz sounded irritable.

"I'm afraid I've no idea, so I haven't." I was really getting into the part. Jack frowned ferociously and mouthed 'Don't overdo it'.

"Well, Miss whatsit, it's very inconvenient, tell Mr. Polstetter this had better be a matter of vital importance. I'll be there in half an hour." The receiver was slammed down. My ear reverberated.

"He went for it." We hugged each other.

Jack suddenly stopped and said, "I'm wondering if we should contact Sergeant Jones. After all he is looking for the man."

"Oh no," I did my pout. "Let's wait until we find out where he's living. Then take it from there. While we're waiting, why don't we have another go at the notebook? I've had a few thoughts on that."

Chapter Fourteen

Never did a half hour pass so slowly. We sat studying the notebook, and talking back and forth, but we weren't interested in what we were doing.

Eventually Jack glanced at his watch (yes, that watch), and said, "He's not coming by the look of things."

He'd barely got the words out when Collins/Fitz appeared. Walking briskly and looking as if he meant business.

"How about we creep up to the shop, then you can....." I started to say, but Jack held up his hand.

"There's going to be no creeping anywhere, and that's final."

We sat watching the entrance. I longed to be over there listening in, but I didn't dare to move. Jack would have killed me.

After what seemed like forever, but was only ten minutes, Collins emerged and stormed – yes, definitely stormed off in the direction he had come.

Jack started the car, and very carefully we drove after Collins. Luckily, there was just enough traffic to act as cover. At any other time I would have enjoyed studying the architecture and surroundings, but not today. About half way down the street, Collins stopped and unlocked his car. As he pulled away we followed cautiously.

My knowledge of Cheltenham was very sketchy, so if asked I couldn't have said where we were or even where we'd been. Collins kept his speed strictly regulated. Slowing on the approach to traffic lights well in advance, cornering steadily, keeping well to his side of the road. Almost as if he was deliberately letting us shadow him. But he couldn't have been, surely. We'd been very careful – and were not strangers to this kind of surveillance.

Presently we had left the city behind, and were travelling at a steady pace along a dual carriageway. After a while I began to recognise the road signs. We were en route to The Flowerdew, I was sure of it. Jack must have thought so too, because he began whistling. Not loud piercing whistling, more, under his breath.

However, Collins suddenly pulled into the driveway of smallish detached house, one of several similar. We kept going, until we had negotiated a bend. Jack parked, and we sprinted back in the direction of the house.

By the time we arrived and were peering carefully round the gateposts, Collins had disappeared.

"What shall we do now?" I asked Jack, who was going at that lip again.

"See if it's possible to get round the back," he said, "I thought I noticed a footpath a few yards down."

Holding our breath we made a dash across the entranceway then hared down to the possible footpath. The path looked as though it skirted the backs of the row of houses. They had probably been built in the 1970's.

"How shall we know which one is his," I asked Jack, as we crept along the path. "I didn't think to count them."

"Don't worry. It's a good thing one of us has their mind on the job."

From the back the house looked very ordinary. There was a conservatory, with French doors leading onto an area of decking, and a garden laid mainly to lawn, and some flowerbeds with a beautiful array of blooms. All in all there was nothing to suggest that this was the home of a criminal mastermind.

We lurked outside, keeping low behind the hedge. I couldn't help wishing that I'd brought our binoculars, but it was going to be eyes only.

'Four Eyes Everywhere'. Jack's idea. What a stupid name. I'm going to change it as soon as we get home, no matter what Jack says, I thought.

The French doors were open, and I squinted hard, to try and see the room beyond the conservatory. It was no good, the sunshine made the interior too dark.

Presently, a woman emerged from the house, she was probably the one who'd answered the phone. She was plump and pleasant looking, her white hair cut in a fashionable bob.

There was a small table with four chairs on the decking, she sat down and called, "Fitz, hurry up with that drink, I'm dying of thirst," this was followed by a peal of laughter.

Fitz came out a few seconds later carrying a tray with a pitcher of Pimms.

Oh, for goodness sake, I thought, now I'm dying of thirst.

Fitz sat at the table and poured two large glassfuls. Mrs. Fitz (if that was who she was) took a long swallow and sighed with pleasure.

"Thank God, you've nearly finished this last job," she said. I don't know about Jack, but I certainly pricked up my ears.

"Shall you be back to normal, after this? That's if you can call your job 'normal'."

Fitz also took a long swallow, then dabbed his lips with an immaculate pocket handkerchief.

"Yes, love," he said. "It will be back in the old routine. We can settle down into doing what we do best for the forseeable future."

He's obviously got big score, and he's going to slide into his cover again. This and other thoughts were jostling for position in my head.

"I don't know why you were chosen anyway," the woman said. "You're getting too long in the tooth for this sort of caper."

So he's not Mr.X, I thought, he gets his orders from above. This must be some organisation he's working for. Diamonds, murders, jewellers on the take – wowee!

Jack was holding his watch up, straining to catch every word.

An hour must have passed, and my knees felt as though they had turned to cement. Jack kept changing his watch from one side to the other, grimacing as he did so. We hadn't heard much of the conversation, perhaps it was the drink, but their voices had become more muted.

Eventually, for which I was thankful, the pair returned indoors.

Jack and I shuffled backward for a few yards and struggled to our feet.

"I don't think I shall ever walk properly again," I moaned. "All my toes are cracked, possibly even broken, and as for my knees....."

"Stop whingeing," Jack said, "this was all your idea, remember? I wanted to contact Sergeant Jones, but you wouldn't have it, oh no, always think you can do better......" He rambled on in this vein for several seconds, until we had reached the end of the footpath.

We hobbled back to the car, and I've never been so glad to sit down in my life.

"Let's get back The Flowerdew and have a drink," I begged. "I'm sure my tongue's turned to sandpaper."

"Hmph," was all Jack said, but nevertheless, he drove off rapidly. The roads were clear, so it wasn't too long before we were ensconced in the bar sipping our libations.

"Come on, don't keep me in suspense, let's hear what they were saying," I was on the edge of my chair.

Jack twiddled around for a few seconds then nodded. I leaned forward feeling excited. The couple had been speaking softly, almost secretively, so there was a good chance that we would be privy to something incriminating.

We listened intently for ten minutes, then sat back and looked at each other. The most incriminating thing we'd heard, was that Fitz was going all out to beat his neighbour's roses this year, at the flower show.

Jack fast forwarded and we had another listen, this time it was their son-in-law in the firing line. He couldn't turn his hand to anything in the house, made a complete pig's ear of everything – nearly blew the place up when he tried to re-wire a plug!

"What is all this," I said to Jack, in despair.

"Search me," he said. "It could be any married couple just chewing the fat. I wouldn't be his son-in-law for anything, the poor bloke must be a bundle of nerves."

"One thing's for sure," I said, "we've got nothing of any value at all. What a waste of time, and please don't say it's all my fault."

"He's a skilled operator," Jack said. "With his background and appearance, no one would ever suspect he was anything other than what he seems."

We sat silent, feeling quite depressed. I had been so sure that we were on the right track, but Fitzgerald was smart. Oh lordy, I suddenly had a dreadful thought.

"Jack," I said, "d'you think that Fitz knows we're on to him, and is laying a trail to lure us in?"

"It had crossed my mind," my dear husband said. "I wasn't happy when we were creeping about outside his property, it was all too easy."

I closed my eyes and tried not to panic. All I could think was, two murders already, and we were nicely placed to be two more.

"Perhaps we should ring Sergeant Jones. Like now?" I whispered.

Jack looked at me. "All of a sudden she wants to make friends with the law," he said, to no-one in particular. "You've changed your tune, haven't you?"

"Well, I don't see what else we can do. Perhaps we ought to pass over the notebook, it's obvious that we can't do anything with it." I sat there feeling a complete idiot.

"We'll give this recorder, one more go," Jack said. "We're nearly at the end anyway."

As we listened, we heard what we couldn't have heard when we were behind the hedge. The sound of a phone ringing.

Fitz said, "That'll be the boss, he'll have got a bit of follow-up for me with any luck, then I...." but what he was saying faded away.

"That's it," I said, a little louder than I should have. Jack put a finger to his lips, ssshing me.

"That's it," I said again, very softly. "The big score is obviously coming. Let's get onto Sergeant Jones, he'll want to know about this."

We finished our drinks and left the bar. The young honeymoon couple were just coming in. The husband put his arm round his young wife and kissed her on the cheek. He smiled, and tipped his head as if to say, 'how about us then?'

We smiled as we made our way upstairs. "Honeymooners. Ah, those were the days." Jack said.

Once in our room, Jack wasted no time ringing the Sergeant's number.

After the initial 'how are you's' he proceeded to give a little run down on what we'd been doing. I couldn't hear the exact response, but there seemed to be a bit of high pitched sound. Almost as if someone was yelling.

Jack sat holding the phone as if it were red hot, saying, "Yes, yes of course. No, no certainly not. Oh, by the way, no never mind it'll keep, so sorry. We'll be there very soon, humble apologies."

He looked at me. "He was not best pleased with us Pippsy. We may have overstepped the mark this time. We've to go to the station as soon as poss, tales between legs, eat humble pie, the lot. I don't know quite what's going on, but something surely is, and we could have poked our noses in the wrong place!"

Chapter Fifteen

At the station we sat waiting for about fifteen minutes, trying not to look at anyone who passed through. I could feel Jack beginning to get restless. Shifting from side to side on his chair, and crossing and uncrossing his legs.

"Sit still," I whispered. "You look guilty."

"I bloody feel guilty," he whispered back. "How much longer are we going to be here?"

There was a constant passage of people through the entrance. Some made for the stairs, others for a door marked 'Private – CID only'.

At last the door opened and Sergeant Jones strode out.

"Mr. and Mrs. Standage, come this way please."

We crept after him, trying to look as small and innocent as we could. I couldn't help thinking that for a Police station purporting to have only three officers, there was an awful lot of activity.

The sergeant pointed to a couple of chairs in front of a desk littered with papers. A computer was situated on a table to the side, with three filing cabinets on the back wall. He seated himself behind the desk, rustled a few sheets of paper, before looking at us.

"So," he said, "what on earth did you think you were doing?"

As I opened my mouth, Jack quickly said, "We spotted the man calling himself Inspector Collins, as I said on the phone, and it seemed important to find out just exactly where he was hiding. So to speak, that is. If we had waited to ring you, we could have lost him."

"Very plausible, Mr. Standage. Did it occur to you to make a note of the car registration? No. Did you think of calling us as you tailed it? No. Did you think of ringing us when you reached the house? No. For two intelligent people, and I assume that you are intelligent, you have behaved in an extremely irresponsible manner."

He paused, then continued, "You could have caused wall to wall problems by your interference, and almost made an important operation go exceedingly sour."

Jack and I sat there, listening and wondering what was going on.

"Ever since the first body was discovered, you have been there or thereabouts poking and prying. Fortunately, the situation has been retrieved somewhat, but not before I was severely reprimanded by my superiors, who, I may say, will be wanting to have a little talk with you by and by."

I felt my legs turn to jelly, it seemed we really had put our feet in it this time. I wished with all my heart that we had ignored the whole episode, and just acted like ordinary people do.

We heard the door behind us open, and shrank down in our chairs. A voice we both recognised said, "Well, well, well, Mr. and Mrs. Standage, you are ubiquitous are you not?"

It was Fitzgerald/Collins.

My first and abiding thought was, we got the whole story wrong from start to finish.

"You will be wondering why I'm here, and not banged up for murder, robbery or other heinous crimes I'm quite sure. Let me introduce myself, I am Superintendant Arthur Fitzgerald, and I am working in an undercover capacity with regard to the activities which have occurred in and around these environs."

Jack and I had no inkling what to say or do, so we just sat there, staring at the Superintendant, I supposed we must think of him that way, and waited for his next pronouncement.

"I propose to put you in the picture as far as I feel able, as you have seen fit to involve yourselves. My brief was to introduce myself as the investigating officer for the apparent murder of the man found outside The Flowerdew Hotel. I knew the man, Mr. Harry Purvis, was here to meet and negotiate with the representative of someone who wished to acquire certain precious stones. We all know that Mr. Carmichael was that representative, but was in the invidious position of having neither the stones, nor the money which would have been payment.

"We now know that you, Mr. and Mrs. Standage, had found the stones and had made up a scenario to fit what you thought had happened. Perhaps your motives were well intentioned, but nevertheless, it seems incredible that you persisted in your interference, after you had given me the stones. Involving the local police was no doubt public spirited in your minds, but as a result I have had to break my cover in order to attempt to unravel some of the complications which have resulted.

"What you have blundered into, is far bigger than you could possibly imagine. The diamonds and the suitcaseful of bank notes are side issues. The murders which occurred were unfortunate of course, but quite incidental. The victims were minor irritations, to be dealt with as swiftly as possible, to clear the way as it were. Though whoever beat the man who was placed in the field, was obviously a vicious thug. That poor soul, I am at liberty to tell you, had been acting as a bodyguard to Mr. Purvis, another poor soul, who was in the wrong place at the wrong time."

Jack and I had sat in silence throughout the Superintendant's lecture. Although I was annoyed that we'd gone so badly wrong in our assessment of the situation, I was still convinced that we had a trump card up our sleeves, in the shape of the notebook. I was, however, not looking forward to confessing to that transgression.

Superintendant Fitzgerald cleared his throat, then said, "We are still uncertain, exactly who are responsible for the murders, and where they fit into the overall picture. Now, if you have anything further you would like to tell me, this is the time."

I opened my bag and produced the notebook.

Both the Superintendant and Sergeant Jones leaned forward.

"Where did you find this, young lady?" The Superintendant asked, rather quietly.

"Well, as a matter of fact, it was in the suitcase with the money. I was astonished that you hadn't discovered it. I mean, we had every intention of giving it to you, well, that is, if not you then probably Sergeant Jones, but we've been a bit busy and everything......oh dear."

I tailed off, it all sounded so pathetic. Had I been able I would have crawled under my chair and stayed there.

Superintendant Fitzgerald held out his hand, into which I put the book.

"You will, of course, have examined what is written within?" he said.

We nodded in unison.

"And what was your conclusion?"

"That we couldn't make any sense of it. We thought it might be some sort of code, but if it is, we aren't smart enough to decipher it." Jack had found his voice at last.

"You do yourselves a disservice Mr. Standage." Fitzgerald's lips twitched. "I think, had you persisted, you would have been able to come up with a solution. However, it is not your concern any longer. I would suggest that you make your way back to your hotel, and settle down to enjoying the rest of your holiday. A suggestion, I believe I made to you once before."

"Dead on Arrival
"

"Dead on Arrival
"

Chapter Sixteen

We didn't talk much on the way back to the hotel. I think we both felt deflated, added to which I felt a total idiot.

Jack's right I thought, I go rushing in without thinking everything through. I get an idea in my head, and as he so rightly says, I won't allow for any other solution.

Back at the hotel we made for the watering hole. All this drinking at odd times - we'll be a couple of alkies before this is over I thought.

However, after sitting sipping for a while I had to put into words an odd feeling that I just could not shake off.

"Jack hon, can I run something by you - just for the record?"

Jack raised an enquiring eyebrow, but didn't say anything.

"It's this," I began. "Whatever he might have said, don't you think that Fitzgerald is the wrong rank to be 'undercover' as he put it? I thought that officers whose job it was to work undercover were usually sergeants or something, and a good bit younger than he is, to boot?"

Jack took a swallow of his malt.

"You could be right, Pips," he said. "Funnily enough, I was thinking something similar myself."

"And," I added for good measure, "we still don't know who phoned him. Unless, of course there's someone else in the equation that we haven't sussed yet?"

"Pippsy," there was a warning note in Jack's voice. "We've been ordered to butt out, and I thought that's what we both wanted. Now you're starting all over again."

"No, I'm not, really I'm not, it's just those two little points are niggling me."

He sighed, as though the weight of the world was on his shoulders – perhaps he thought it was. I'm sure I drive him to the edge of reason sometimes.

"At least let's attempt to find out who made the phone call." I wheedled. I do quite a good wheedle, so I hoped it would work.

Jack sighed again.

"Anything to shut you up. We'll have a chat with Caroline, see if she remembers who it was, and if needs be, ask the Barnsworths. But, Pippsy, that's it – end of story."

He's gorgeous when he gets all macho – I wished we were in our room – but first things first.

We drank up and strolled over to Reception. Caroline bustled out of the office, all professional smiles.

"How may I help?" she said.

"Caroline, you were in the hall during the shermozzle the other evening. Robert was hollering for someone to call the police, can you recall who did?" Jack smiled.

She creased her beautifully made up, unlined brow. Caroline in thinking mode I supposed. I mentally rapped my knuckles for being bitchy.

"I think," she said at last. "I think it was Mr. Crichton, he's one of the single gentlemen who are here at the moment. I believe he's travelling on business, and has several appointments in this area."

Bingo, I thought. Mr. Crichton eh, I wonder which one he is?

Jack must have had the same thought, as he asked, "Could you point him out at dinner this evening, it would be really helpful?"

He smiled his killer smile again, looking even more gorgeous.

Caroline crumbled at once (they always do). "It would be a pleasure to help you Mr. Standage, any time." (I'll bet it would, I thought).

"By the way," I put in my two centsworth. "How's Robert now? He's found it tough going recently hasn't he?"

Caroline tore her eyes away from Jack, and looked at me unenthusiastically.

"He's coping, just about, but he had to visit the doctor to get something for his nerves. I'm sure he'll be fine when all this upset is over."

So shall all of us, darling, I thought, as we thanked her and moved away.

That evening Caroline was as good as her word. She moved discreetly through the dining room, greeting guests as she passed by and pausing briefly at a table where a single blonde-haired man was sitting. A slight nod, as she looked in our direction was all that was required. Then she glanced around the room, as if checking to make sure that all was as it should be, before disappearing back into the hall.

"That's our man," I said, "and he's blonde, which is why I confused him with Mr. Yogurt."

We sat enjoying our meal, and keeping an eye on Mr. Crichton. He was tucking into his dinner as though he hadn't eaten recently, plus downing a bottle of Merlot at an alarming rate.

He called for a second bottle, and we overheard, "All on expenses. Might as well make the most of it – ha ha ha."

The waiter smiled weakly – he'd heard it all before.

We thought he was going to sit there all night. Eventually, however, he stood up, a tad unsteadily perhaps, and made his way to the bar - and I'd thought we were knocking it back a bit!

After a discreet interval we followed him. Ignoring the waves and smiles from the Barnsworths, we perched on stools at the bar, alongside him.

"What are you drinking?" Jack asked. I was about to say "my usual", when I realised that Jack was talking to Crichton.

"That's very civil of you, old man," was the answer, "a large brandy, if you don't mind?"

Once we were all furnished with drinks, Jack asked casually, "Are you a frequent visitor here?"

"No, this is my first time. Pretty good billet though, just a shame that I'm here on business. Have to come back and bring the little woman."

He was the archetypal business man away from home. A little too much so, for my money though.

Jack must have thought the same, because he said, "What sort of business are you in Mr. er er...?"

"Car.....er Crichton. Bill Crichton, nearly forgot my own name then, ha ha ha!"

We sat waiting, Bill Crichton (?) said, "You were asking me about my business, of course. I watch, that is I'm in watches. Pocket watches, very rare and unusual."

"I'd love to see some. I've always been fascinated by timepieces. Repeaters, half-hunters and the like." Jack was really away. I was impressed.

Crichton's face had taken on a glazed expression. I could see he'd no idea what Jack was talking about.

"Yes, well, when I've got more time ha ha ha, have to keep them in the hotel safe you know. Wouldn't do for me to get careless." Crichton was flannelling like mad. He was no more a salesman for rare watches than I was.

My instincts were raring to go. This Crichton, if that was his name, which I doubted after his earlier slip, was tied into the murder/diamond business somewhere.

Jack said, again acting casual, "How about all that upheaval the other evening? Poor Robert hasn't recovered yet. We never did find out who rang the police. I mean, they came so swiftly it was amazing. Don't get a rapid response like that where we live."

Crichton began to look a bit shifty. "Yes, they did come smartly. Actually, I think it was me that rang, I thought it was best.....so much confusion and stuff, someone had to do something?" He ended on a note of enquiry.

"Yes indeed, Mr. Crichton," Jack said. "Your modesty does you credit. How did you know whom to ring?"

"Oh well, I just dialled 999 of course," decidedly shifty now.

"Come, come Mr. Crichton, we both know that 999 was the last number you would have rung."

"I don't know what you mean," he began to bluster. "I just behaved like a good citizen, and did my duty."

"You quite patently did your duty, Mr. Crichton, but not by ringing 999."

Suddenly Crichton changed completely. He dropped the hearty voice, and ceased to bluster.

"Mr. Standage," he said quietly, "I know my boss has told you to keep out of this, so I'm advising you not to persist with these questions. Suffice it to say that we have the matter well in hand, and we don't need a couple of bumbling amateurs throwing a spanner in the works. Do I make myself clear?"

His slightly menacing tone made me shiver. I noticed too, that his one over the eight act had disappeared, along with the other mannerisms.

Whatever he is, I thought, I wouldn't like to get on his wrong side. All the same, I took great exception to his description of us as bumbling amateurs.

I thought that was that, but to my astonishment Jack said, "Mr. Crichton, if that is your name, my wife and I have assisted the police on several previous occasions. That means, we are not amateurs, bumbling or otherwise. Now wouldn't it be useful if we kept our eyes and ears open among the guests for anything untoward? No one would suspect us now, would they? Besides, the police are always asking for members of the public to help them, am I right?"

Crichton, burst out laughing.

"Mr. Standage, your nerve is greater than your common sense. I'm sure you've realised that the operation in progress is extremely dangerous. People have been murdered, and there's no guarantee that there won't be more. D'you really expect us to keep an eye on you, as well as doing the job we're paid for?"

"You don't need to watch out for us," I said. "We'd be very careful. We've got no desire to end up lying on a mortuary slab."

He looked us over for a minute or two, then rather to my surprise he said, "Alright, I'll have a word with the boss. If he gives it the go ahead, I'll let you know what you should do. But in the meanwhile, please, just go to bed." His voice took on a note of near despair.

Chapter Seventeen

We had a slightly restless night. I couldn't believe that Jack had been the one to get us back into the fray. That is if Crichton's boss, whom we suspected was Superintendant Fitzgerald, would agree to us lending a hand.

Actually, I felt quite excited. After the despondency we had felt on leaving the police station, the thought that maybe we would see some action was really stimulating. So much so, in fact, that I leapt out of bed, dragged the clothes off Jack and began poking him in the stomach.

"Oy, oy, what the bloody hell are you doing?" he was pink and cross.

"Come on, slug-a-bed, show a leg, we're going to do some detecting." I was glowing with anticipation.

"We're not going to do anything, until we get the go ahead." Jack still looked cross.

"That's just a formality. We'll get permission, just you wait and see." I felt elated. Jack on the other hand, obviously did not.

Nevertheless, he crawled out of bed and tottered into the shower.

"You don't mind if I have first go, do you?" he called.

I didn't. I had grabbed a sheet of hotel notepaper and was scribbling down what I thought should be our plan of action.

Number one, check up on the other guests. Even the foursome, I decided. The yogurt sales act could be just that, an act.

We had a slight uneasiness about the Barnsworths. Were they or were they not all they seemed to be.

Mr. Jankowsky and his ladyfriend would certainly bear looking at.

There was the other 'businessman', and the family of four.

Oh, and of course, the honeymooners. Though to be honest, I thought they were non-starters. Still, if we were going to do a proper job, then we should give them a look.

By this time Jack emerged from the shower, looking less cross.

"What are you up to?" he said.

"I'm making a list of the people we should have a look at," I told him. "You give it a going over while I shower, then when Crichton or somebody gives us the nod we're all prepared."

Jack shook his head, "I do hope you're not going to have a terrible disappointment."

"Tell you what," I answered, "if they don't want us, we'll carry on anyway, and blow the lot of them." With that I flounced, yes, quite definitely flounced into the shower, leaving Jack laughing fit to burst.

After breakfast on going through my bag, I found the sheet of paper with the details from the notebook. For no real reason I studied them for a moment. Then it hit me – what a dope I was. I looked steadily down the page. Number 162 occurred several times. Sometimes on one day, at hourly intervals. I began to laugh.

Jack was cleaning his teeth in the en suite, but popped his head out and enquired, "What's up?"

"These days and numbers and things, in the notebook – they're TV programmes." I laughed again.

"What are you on about?" Jack finished his teeth and came into the bedroom. "What TV programmes?"

"A little while ago, when business was a bit slack – we got hooked into a TV series, didn't we? Do you remember which one, and which channel?" I sat there looking smug.

Jack thought for a moment then snapped his fingers.

"Yes," he said, "'Law and Order' on channel 162, wasn't it?"

"Well," I said, "just you cast your eye over this list."

He took the paper and began reading. His expression became one of surprise.

"You're right I think, Pippsy. But why on earth would he have a list of TV programmes in a notebook?"

"Could be he was as hooked on them as we were," I suggested. "The book's a reminder to record them or something."

"It seems a bit odd, but yes you're right. There are a few other numbers and times, but all the numbers equate to TV channels. I wonder if old Fitz and the gang will spend hours trying to decipher it." He started to laugh too.

"Why don't we ring them, and say we've cracked the code?" I said.

"No, let's leave it a while. See if they get in touch with us, it'll certainly be a topic of conversation."

After breakfast we sat in the lounge for a while, deciding how to spend our day. For my part I was wondering if we would receive the 'go ahead' call.

Finally, we went for a stroll in the substantial grounds. There was a delightful little walled garden tucked away in one corner, and despite the fact that neither Jack nor I really know one plant from another, we found it charming and restful.

"Wouldn't it be nice," I said, "to have a house in the country with a garden like this. We could run the business from home, and have all the benefits of living away from the city. Perhaps we should have a look at some of the villages around here, what d'you think?"

Jack shook his head. "Pippsy, you're a city girl born and raised. The rural life, I fancy, wouldn't satisfy you for long. But then," he screwed up his eyes, "maybe it would. If we went on running the business, we'd be getting up to London fairly frequently. D'you know, I think you might have got something there."

We linked hands and wandered among the pretty flowerbeds. The more I thought about it, the more I liked it.

My parents after all, had been very keen gardeners, and although we'd lived in the suburbs there'd been a dear little courtyard garden. Maybe I could learn about plants. Mum was in sheltered housing now, since Dad died, but she had a little garden which always looked picture perfect.

"When we get home," Jack said, "we'll get some details from estate agents, and give it serious thought."

"How about we go for a little drive round, just to suss out likely places?" I said.

With that, we walked back to the car, and were just climbing in when we heard our names being called.

We looked round to see Crichton running down the steps.

"Can you spare a minute?" he asked. "Come back in if you will. Shan't keep you long."

We followed him back up the steps and into the Lounge.

"Would you like a drink, coffee or something?" he said.

I was minded to say, "Yes, a large G and T please." But of course, I didn't. We accepted coffee, then sat down and settled back.

This is it, I thought. We're going to be co-opted into the CID.

Unfortunately, it didn't quite come to that, but at least we were given something to do.

"As I understand it, you've done this type of work before?" Crichton said. We nodded.

"Now I know," he went on, "you've been mingling with the guests. In particular, the mature lady and gentleman, the....."

he fished in his pocket for a notebook. "The Barnsworths, am I correct?" Why are the police so stilted in their conversation on occasions?

We nodded again.

"What was your impression of them?" he sat back and looked at us.

"I, that is, we, thought they were perhaps a bit over the top in their efforts to be 'North Country', almost as if they were acting the parts." No point in beating about the bush I thought.

He smiled at me. He had a nice smile. Not like Jack's of course, but then Jack's a one off.

"You're quite astute aren't you Mrs. Standage? The couple in question are in fact... (I held my breath excitedly), actors, getting into character for their parts in a popular TV series. They're new to the series, and as they both hail from London, they've needed to practise their personas a bit."

What a blow. I was expecting him to say that they were well known con artists or something.

So we could cross them off the list.

"Don't be downhearted though," he continued, "there are other guests about whom we would like your opinions." He really is stilted, I thought.

Jack spoke up, and I could have killed him on the spot.

"My dear wife had the idea that a foursome of well dressed guests were not all they appeared. So much so, that she followed two of them one morning, when they seemed to be behaving suspiciously. It turned out that they were in the business of producing yogurt in mixed flavours, and were completing a business transaction with a client. No......" he said as Crichton opened his mouth, "I'm not going to tell you how she discovered this."

I felt my face turn scarlet.

"Ah, Mrs. Standage," Crichton said. "Don't be embarrassed – we all make bloomers from time to time. Even my boss, and," he added confidentially, "I've been known to make a couple."

If all that was meant to make me feel better – it didn't!

"Now. What about anyone else? So far, that is."

"There's a supposed Hollywood producer, a Mr. Jankowsky, he seems a bit suspect, and the father in a family group, but apart from them and of course Carmichael, we're a bit stuck." Jack was at the lip again.

"The boss seems quite happy for you to nose about a bit, but don't be obvious," Crichton said.

"No, no, no, we'll be discretion itself," we assured him.

He stood up, "Thank you for your time, you may be certain that we shall keep a weather eye out for you." He smiled, and strode off headed goodness knows where, but looking purposeful.

I hugged myself with delight.

"I told you we'd get the nod, didn't it? Even if you did make me look a complete berk." I wasn't going to let him off too easily.

"We should try and make a few subtle approaches to Jankowsky. Though quite how we do it eludes me at the moment," Jack said.

"Perhaps, we could try through the girlfriend?" I said. "I can ask about her make up or hair or something. Yes hair, that's the thing. She would certainly believe that I could use tips on that."

Jack looked at me. "Yes, you could get away with that alright."

Ouch! I thought. From my husband of all people, how could he?

"We'll wait until dinner tonight then wing it." It wouldn't be the first time, I thought. "Meanwhile, let's take that drive, and try and spot our future home."

Chapter Eighteen

We spent the rest of the day touring around. The weather was a bit in and out, so it was no real hardship to be in the car.

Several picture postcard villages took our fancy, and we found ourselves becoming more and more excited by the idea of an equally picture postcard home. After noting a few likely looking places, we returned to The Flowerdew feeling upbeat.

"First thing we do when we get back, is tackle the estate agents." I was aglow.

So much so, that I suggested we had a little tipple in the bar before dinner. I'd almost forgotten our mission for the evening I was so full of country houses, and thoughts of a new life.

Jack was all business, however. As we sat with our pre-prandials, he kept a careful watch on who came and went. One or two new people had arrived, and we didn't want to be distracted.

At last Mr. Jankowsky and his lady swept in. Well, at least, she swept, he plodded in her wake. I wondered what they found to talk about. But then, perhaps they didn't do much talking.

She was braying something at him, while he looked as if he needed a stiff drink or several.

Now, how shall we play this, I wondered? I gave Jack a nudge, and stood up taking my drink with me. Jack followed.

As we passed the couple, I stopped and beamed as sincerely as I could.

"Haven't I seen you before?" I said, then thought, idiot, of course you have – here!

"On TV was it?" I said swiftly.

She looked up at me, as she was sitting she was forced to do that.

"I've been in a couple of commercials," she said.

Lucky guess, I thought. "Yes I knew I'd seen you. I admired your hair so much."

That got her, she started into a long complicated description of the process of preparing hair for TV commercials. I stood there trying to look interested, but in reality waiting for Jack to make his move. Which at last, he did.

"Now what are you both drinking?" he said heartily.

Mr. Jankowsky suddenly looked as though he'd won first prize in the lottery.

"I'll have a double bourbon on the rocks, thanks," he said.

"A very dry martini for me. With a olive please." His girlfriend said. "A olive's so surfissicated, aren't it?"

I could really understand Mr. Jankowsky's expression now. Any conversation they had must resemble a pre-school reading book. One could almost feel sorry for him – almost.

"May we sit?" I asked politely.

"Please do, please do," Mr. Jankowsky was brightening up by the second.

Jack came back with the drinks, including another round for us. I must definitely go on the wagon when we get home, I thought.

I engaged the girlfriend, who said her name was Scarlett, in what could just about be called conversation. She finished her diatribe about hair, and started on body make-up, something about which I knew nothing and cared about even less. Scarlett seemed to find it rivetting, as she described anything and everything pertaining to the subject.

Jack meanwhile was discussing hotel accommodation, restaurants, holiday destinations, obviously anything he could think of to pick up clues.

At last he ran out of things to say, and sat sipping his drink. Mr. Jankowsky meanwhile had ordered another couple of rounds, even though Jack and I had insisted we couldn't possibly manage another drop on empty stomachs.

Scarlett was having no problems. She downed two or three, without any apparent effect, and kept talking, about body waxing this time.

I couldn't take it, in more ways than one.

"We really must go in to dinner, I'm starving," I said, trying to keep the beam going. What I was thinking was that I would be paralytic in very short order if I didn't get some food into me.

By the time we sat down, I felt decidedly wobbly, and Jack had a slightly glazed expression.

"My godfathers, how does he stand it?" Jack said.

"Search me. I nearly cracked my jaw trying not to yawn. Between that and the booze, I thought I was going to pass out."

We looked at each other and shrugged. Jack said, "About the only thing I learned was that he's trying to raise finance to make a musical. He reckons he'd be onto a winner if he could get the cash – wants a big player to divvy up. I thought he was going to put the bite on me, but I think he soon realised I wasn't in the big league so to speak. It looks as though he is what he purports to be – a producer; but Hollywood he ain't."

The dinner we ordered would definitely not have figured in a Weight Watchers recipe book, but we thought it politic, to soak up the alcohol.

"One thing," I said. "That's another one crossed off the list. Unless Scarlett is the big brain behind everything, and he's just there for window dressing."

Jack almost choked on his dinner roll, and I had to stand up and pat his back. By the time he'd finished laughing, thankfully, the main course had arrived.

Our fulsome dinner left us extremely full. However, it had dissipated the effects of the booze somewhat. We wandered into the lounge and ordered coffee, not even tempted by the thought of brandy.

I looked around, feeling somnolent and relaxed. The Barnsworths were enjoying tea and biscuits of all things! Neither Jack nor I felt we could face any more 'eh up' or 'ee ba gum', most particularly as we knew it was all play acting, so we closed our eyes and pretended to doze.

Nature took over from pretence, at least for me. I must have really slept, because I suddenly jerked upright at the sound of – what?

Jack too looked as though he had enjoyed forty winks. He caught my eye, "Did you just hear something odd?"

I dropped my head and shook it, to clear my thoughts. "There was a...a...noise. A scream or shout, something like that."

We looked round the room, the Barnsworths were on their feet, and several other guests appeared perturbed. The foursome who must have come in after we'd dropped off, looked as though their eyes were going to start out of their heads.

Jack and I stood up and walked into the foyer. There we found Robert stretched out on the floor, and Caroline having mild hysterics outside the office door.

Caroline calmed down considerably at the sight of Jack, until she proceeded to burst into tears.

"What's the problem?" Jack asked, as I patted her back and said, "There, there."

"The office – in the office – I think he's, he's dead!"

"Dead, who's dead?" Jack and I chorused.

"In..in..there. Oh, it's terrible, I can't believe all this is happening, I shall hand in my notice after this." She was pale and unsteady.

"You take a seat. Have some brandy. Put your head between your knees – you'll be fine in a moment." We tried to reassure her.

While she was collapsing into a chair, and calling for a waiter, Jack and I made our way to the office. The door was ajar, so we pushed it open and saw the body on the floor. Eyes staring, tongue protruding, obviously strangled with his own tie, poor Carmichael for once in his life was not pale of face.

I turned away, but Jack knelt down and went through the motions of feeling his pulse.

"I think it might be an idea to track Crichton down," he said. "I didn't notice him at dinner, but he may just have eaten early."

We left the office, and Jack pulled the door closed behind us.

Robert was now sitting up in a chair sipping a drink, while Caroline was receiving hand pattings and face moppings from Dolly Barnsworth.

"Is it bad?" Arnold asked, with no trace whatsoever of a North Country accent.

"Pretty bad," Jack replied. "Have you by any chance seen Mr. Crichton? He's one of the businessmen here on his own."

"As a matter of fact, I have," he said. "He drove off about half an hour ago. You were spark out at the time. Why? Do you think he's connected somehow?"

"To that, I have no answer," Jack told him. "But it would be useful if we knew where he was going. I think I'll ring the local station. We'll have to do that anyway – seeing as we've got another murder on our hands."

There was a loud groan from Robert, who sat slumped in his chair.

"I can't go on. I am on the verge of a breakdown. Three bodies, my career in tatters and my nerves in shreds. Why me? That's what I want to know." He closed his eyes and put his hand to his throat.

"Get a grip Robert. It could have been worse – not much perhaps, but still the police will handle it all." I did my best, but he was beyond reason. Robert's not at his best in a crisis I thought, even if all that's happened is over the top.

Jack was busily dialling the police.

His conversation with Sergeant Jones was fairly brief and to the point. I could have sworn I heard a groan from the end of the line.

"The good Sergeant assured me he would be here with all speed," Jack said. Then grinning, he added, "I think he's feeling the strain a little."

The aforementioned good Sergeant arrived very quickly indeed. We took him to the office, where after one swift glance he rang for back up.

"The Super will be along directly," he said. "And he'll certainly want to talk to you two."

"We did find out that the man calling himself Crichton was part of your set up," Jack said.

"And that Mr. Jankowsky, is just a small time film producer. What about Mr. Crichton, or whatever he's called?" I asked. "I thought he was part of the investigating team?"

Sergeant Jones didn't bat an eyelid. "I'm not at liberty to respond to any questions of that kind," he replied, and strode out of the office.

We also left, and a few minutes later he persuaded Caroline and Robert to provide a few details.

Jack and I wandered into the bar. Why did we always repair to the bar, I asked myself? I gratefully sipped a large G and T while Jack was swallowing a malt, and appeared thankful to be doing so.

We looked up as Superintendant Fitzgerald hove into view. He made a beeline for us and stood, arms folded, looking us over.

"Mr. and Mrs. Standage," he said, "you're beginning to irritate me. 'Four Eyes Everywhere' with the accent on the 'Everywhere'. Plus seemingly leaving a trail of bodies behind you."

"Please, Superintendant, that's not fair," I said indignantly. "We can't help it if corpses keep turning up all over the place."

He sighed, then unfolded his arms and pulled up a chair. "Alright, I shall know no peace of mind, until you tell me what you've discovered. If anything."

I chipped in. "But there are still a few people we haven't looked into yet."

The Superintendant sat silent. Then he looked up.

"I shouldn't really be telling you this, but Crichton is not part of our set up, as you put it. So forget whatever he told you. One thing's certain however, we still haven't discovered who else in this hotel is involved."

For once, I was stunned into silence. So Crichton had fooled us. I wracked my brain trying to recall what we had told him. I was fairly certain that we hadn't mentioned diamonds or money. But why had he asked us to investigate the other guests?

Then of course, it hit me. If we were looking at other guests, we were not looking at him. Doubtless he thought he'd sidelined us very nicely. Which of course, he had.

The Superintendant was looking at me quizzically.

"I imagine, Mrs. Standage, that this man Crichton had persuaded you to focus your attentions in other directions. Am I right?"

"One hundred per cent Superintendant," I told him. "We were about to look at some of the guests we had not previously considered. Hadn't we Jack?" I thought it was about time my husband was drawn into the conversation.

"Absolutely Pippsy," he said on cue.

"If I may be permitted....?" the Superintendant began, "perhaps you would care to apprise me of the guests you were considering."

"Well," I said, "there's a family of four, that don't seem much like a family to me. If they are holidaymakers, the man we assume is the father shows no interest in holidaying at all. He's either not here, or is on the phone when he is here."

"And...?" he continued to look at me.

"We chatted to the so-called film producer and his lady friend, but we think they are just what they appear to be."

"Don't forget the foursome," Jack said with a sly wink.

I could feel my face becoming hot. "We, that is I, was able to eliminate them I think." I didn't expand.

"Apparently, so Crichton said, the Barnsworths – the North Country couple, are in fact actors getting into character for a new TV series, so we eliminated them too," Jack said, sounding very laid back.

The Superintendant listened, never taking his eyes off us.

"The reason we were investigating was because Crichton told us that his boss, whom we assumed was you, thought we could help out without anyone suspecting us." I finished in a rather lame fashion.

"Did you honestly suppose that any self-respecting senior police officer would propose a scenario like that?" The Superintendant shook his head, looking almost sad at such an idea.

He went on, "So far, your powers of deduction have proved limited in the extreme. Each time you make an assumption it's the wrong one. How you've managed to survive in your chosen profession beggars belief. If I suspect for even one minute that you are involving yourselves in this case any further, you will be in serious trouble. Do I make myself clear?"

We couldn't have replied if we'd wanted to. A nod of our heads was all we could manage.

The Superintendant didn't just stand, he rose to his feet. "I trust that you will enjoy the remainder of your holiday." He gave a brief nod and strode out into the foyer, which was awash with official looking people going about their official looking business.

That night as we climbed unsteadily into bed – we'd needed a couple more stiffeners after our encounter with the Superintendant – we agreed that was it. No more investigating. We'd do exactly what had been suggested, and just enjoy the rest of our holiday.

Chapter Nineteen

I woke up with what was becoming my customary hangover. Jack was snoring fit to beat the band.

As I lay there, hoping I could catch a little doze, my mind was still going over our conversation of last evening. I had no intention of disobeying our instructions of course, but all the same that itch was back again, and I did so want to scratch it.

I couldn't stand it any longer. I poked my comatose husband smartly in the ribs.

He groaned and rolled onto his back.

"Wake up, Detective 1st class," I said, with all the determination I could muster. "I can't stand to see this case going on without us. If we poke about a bit more, we can redeem ourselves, I just know it."

Jack was suddenly wide awake.

"I don't believe I heard what I thought I just heard," he said. "Fitzgerald will have us served up on a plate for breakfast. Honestly Pippsy, you're going to have to give up on this one. If you interfere at all, it'll be like the wrath of God, I promise you. And, not just from Fitzgerald either. I shall wring your neck."

"No, just listen a minute," I was feeling the rightness of it all. "We won't interfere as such. We can talk quite innocently to the guests we haven't approached yet. Just discussing the in's and out's of everything that's been happening. We won't look out of place, we'll be socialising that's all."

Jack jumped out of bed and began pummelling the wall.

"No, no, no, my godfathers, what have I married? Have you got a self-destruct button, because you seem about to press it?"

"Calm yourself," I said, which I know infuriates him, but I didn't care. I felt very strongly that I was right.

"We both wanted to find out exactly what was going on. Didn't we? So if we go about it the right way, that's just what we'll do. Come on Jacko, you know you want to."

"I give up, I just give up," he sat down heavily on the bed.

"Now hear this," he went on, "if anything at all goes wrong again, I am disassociating myself from you completely."

"Whoopee Jacko, I knew you'd agree," I leapt onto him and gave him a huge kiss and cuddle.

"You won't get round me that way," he said – but he was smiling. We spent a few minutes having a snog, then on the count of three flung ourselves off the bed, and raced for the shower. As usual Jack won, but credit where it's due I was spared Pavarotti.

At breakfast we discussed our plan of action. I thought we should try tackling the family. It wasn't going to be easy as they were not the friendliest people we'd ever met.

To be honest, I thought that there was little or nothing to be gained by talking to them, but we had to eliminate each and every one. So, as soon as we saw them gathering themselves to leave the dining room, we stood up and sauntered in their direction.

As usual, the children looked sullen, the mother resigned and the father bad tempered. We nodded as we drew level.

"Another lovely morning," I carolled brightly.

The children looked straight through me. The mother had the good grace to respond, but with a distinct lack of enthusiasm.

"Yes, we've been very lucky with the weather."

They made to pass on, but I said even more brightly, "What are you planning to do today?"

The girl snorted and said, "As little as possible. This place is the pits. Nothing to do, nowhere decent to go, and no people worth speaking to."

She and her brother wandered off, while their mother said apologetically, "Teenagers, what can you do?" She moved away, followed by her husband, who was taking out his mobile phone.

"Got calls to make," we heard him say. "I'll see you later."

Jack and I looked after them. "That was a washout if ever there was one," Jack said.

"I don't think they can be mixed up in anything. Even the father. He looks too depressed to be a high flying criminal."

I had to agree. We looked around, but apart from one businessman and the honeymooners the dining room was deserted.

"We'll have to wait until tonight," I said. "Everyone will be either here or in the bar. It could be that some of the people who have just arrived are in the frame."

Jack looked over his shoulder. "What about those three?" he asked.

"Weeell," I said doubtfully, "I expect they're as innocent as we are. Perhaps we'll look them over later on, but I don't hold out any hopes."

"You're probably right," he said. "I don't think the honeymoon couple even know what day it is, let alone what's been happening around them. As for the businessman, it's unlikely that there would be two of them doing the same job. As we've got Crichton as a suspect, that'll do I think."

We'd gone off the boil a little.

"Let's have another trip to Cheltenham," I said. "Or better still, Broadway. I could look at those leather coats I've been hearing about."

Chapter Twenty

In the event there was no leather coat that day. We decided to forego any shopping trips and instead stay close the hotel. I was hoping that we could look over some of the other guests, but unfortunately, unlike us, they all took off.

Even the family piled themselves into their car, with the children, for once, looking more cheerful. Perhaps father had decided some retail therapy might do the trick.

We had a brief stroll around the grounds, and even approached the gate with a view to walking a little further afield. However, neither of us fancied the lane, so we turned back, and went into the bar for a pre-lunch drink.

We sat down to eat (salad for me, fishcakes with saute potatoes and a selection of veggies for Jack), in a practically deserted dining room.

The foursome were parked at their usual table, and appeared to be eating sparingly. They kept their voices low, although there were a couple of bottles of wine on the table, so towards the end of the meal there were a few bursts of laughter.

Only three other tables were occupied, one by a couple I hadn't seen before, and the other two by men on their own. There was no sign of the honeymooners - probably understandable, as their honeymoon so far must have been a bit of a washout.

"Well, today's been a load of nothing up to now," I said. "I don't think there's going to be too much problem keeping out of harm's way at this rate."

We went to our room, and took a nap.

These few days were supposed to be a romantic break, was my last thought, and all we've done is discover bodies, answer questions, and drink too much.

I woke very suddenly, about an hour and a half later. Jack was still sound asleep, but I had an uneasy feeling. What had woken me? Was there a noise, or did my brain remember something and prod me?

Trying to be careful, I slid off the bed and crossed to the door. I stood there, just listening. Then I heard it. Outside our room, there's a creaky floorboard. I pressed my ear against the door. The chances of hearing anything worthwhile were remote. The Flowerdew was once a Victorian mansion, so the walls and doors are thick. Nevertheless, I stayed where I was for a few minutes.

Someone began turning the door handle. I took a few steps back. The door was locked of course, but one never knew!

Now I could distinctly hear voices. Too soft to hear actual words, but there was also a scratching sound around the lock.

The doors at The Flowerdew had old fashioned locks with keys, no new-fangled cards and slots. So I was sure that someone was attempting to pick the lock.

I crept over to the bed, put my hand over Jack's mouth and shook him.

He woke smartly and tried to push my hand away.

"Ssh, don't make a sound," I whispered. "Someone's trying to break into the room."

He lay dead still, and we both strained to hear what was happening. The scratching ceased after a minute or two then the handle was tried again. Luckily, the lock must have been good and strong, because the door refused to open.

There was a further murmur of voices, then the floorboard creaked and the voices faded away.

By this time I was in a sweat, and Jack didn't look too happy either.

"I've got a nasty feeling that whoever was trying to get in, meant us no good," I said shakily.

"It's probable that it was guests that we've not yet eliminated," Jack said. "We're going to have to box clever, or we'll be joining the ranks of the deceased."

I felt my knees go weak, and sat down on the edge of the bed rather quickly.

"It was at least two people out there," I said, "so we'll have to look everyone over very carefully this evening. Do you think we should ring Sergeant Jones, or the Superintendant, I mean they can't blame us surely – we haven't done anything this time?"

"I think we should hold off doing that yet," Jack said positively. "We'll act all bright and innocent tonight to persuade whoever it was, that we don't know a thing."

"Suppose it doesn't work, and they come creeping back in the middle of the night? We could be murdered in our bed." I know my face must have been pale – Jack's certainly was.

"We can't afford to think like that. We've got to remain positive. Tell you what, Pippsy pet, if I feel the slightest doubt this evening I'll have a quiet word with Robert, and get us moved to another room. I think there are a couple still empty."

I shuddered. I pictured what the news would do to Robert, it would finish him off.

After a while we got a hold of ourselves, and tried to think who the would-be intruders could be.

"It must be someone who's been keeping an eye on us," I said. "The idea that it could be a new guest, just doesn't sit right with me."

Jack agreed. "I think you're probably right Pippsy, and it does narrow the field considerably, but the problem is, there are not many likely suspects."

It was my turn to agree, I counted them off on my fingers. "That means it's got to be the other businessman, the foursome, or the honeymooners."

Then despite everything, I laughed and said, "How about a conspiracy between Robert and Caroline?"

Jack said, "It's possible, but somehow I can't see a guy who faints at the mere mention of murder, belonging to the sort of criminal fraternity that this appears to be."

"He'd have to be a very good actor, and somehow he just doesn't come across that way." The slight lightening of the atmosphere did us both good.

"Let's try to keep the booze down tonight, shall we?" I asked. "We're going to have to keep our wits about us."

"Don't worry," Jack assured me, "our wits will be wrapped around us like blankets. Still, I could certainly use a stiff drink – but you're right, we should try and lay off a bit."

So there we were an hour later, sitting in the bar with our usual tipples. My eyes really were Everywhere, each person who entered was given the once over, but so far none of the usual suspects had arrived.

We tried to look casual and kept laughing as we talked, in an effort to appear carefree.

Eventually, we decided to go in to dinner. It was a good move. Within a few minutes a steady stream of familiar faces made their way to their tables. They were all there. Trouble was none of them looked like murderers, or even criminals. But then, I thought, Crichton hadn't looked like anything other than the businessman he purported to be.

One thing was certain, this was not going to be easy. Criminals don't normally advertise themselves.

"Dead on Arrival
"

Chapter Twenty-One

Dinner seemed to go on forever. The waiters bustled about without appearing to achieve much. I suppose one could have some sympathy, after all the misfortunes that had befallen the hotel in the last week. All the same I definitely began to feel antsy, and Jack was not eating with his normal relish.

We declined dessert, and took coffee in the lounge. Attempting to keep our buoyant demeanour going was not easy, and I wished we could just leave and tuck ourselves up in bed. The thought of packing and going home was suddenly very appealing.

The Barnsworths were the first to breeze in. They made a bee-line for us, and my heart sank. I was not in the mood for North Country bonhomie.

However, the sat down and in very subdued voices told us their story.

In the first place, although they were married their names were not Arnold and Dolly, nor even Barnsworth. These apparently, were the names of the characters they would be portraying in the TV series due to start filming in a month.

"We thought that being Londoners we should take a bit of time getting into character." Arnold looked almost shamefaced.

"My name's James Staples by the way, and my wife is Annette Barclay. We work under our own names for professional purposes, and it's only occasionally that we get booked together."

I looked at him carefully, and a vague stirring of recognition came to mind. Had I seen him in something?

"Do you have family?" Jack asked – for something to say, I suspected.

"Yes, as a matter of fact we do," Annette said. "Two daughters, both married, and between them, they've given us three lovely grandchildren. None of them are in the business, although our youngest grandchild did a bit of modelling for Marks and Spencer."

Fearing she was about to launch into a blow by blow description, I quickly asked, "How long is your TV engagement going to last?"

"Well," James said, "we're crossing our fingers it'll be for the entire series – that's eight half hour episodes. It's quite well paid. Very well actually. We hope that if the show proves popular, another series might follow. It could be a pension plan for us, because we'd be able to refuse any work we weren't keen on. In this business you have to take whatever you're offered, just to keep eating regularly."

All of a sudden, they seemed rather pathetic. A mature couple, they must've been in their early sixties, desperately working to provide a modicum of security for the future.

I could sense Jack felt the same, for he said, "Now then, what are you drinking? We must have a toast to your future success as household names."

They smiled at us, and gladly accepted the offer.

The rest of the evening passed pleasantly enough, as we were regaled with tales of their careers over the years. They could tell a good story, and certainly appeared happy enough, but it all seemed like a very hard life to me.

As we went up to bed Jack and I agreed that despite everything that had happened, we would rather be us than James Staples and Annette Barclay.

The evening had not, we thought, been wasted. We felt fairly certain that we could cross the 'Barnsworths' off our list of suspects. Not unless their acting abilities were of Oscar standard. Which seemed doubtful.

All the same, bearing in mind our experience earlier in the day, we locked the door then jammed a chair under the handle.

It took a long while to drop off. Even for Jack, who was usually asleep as his head hit the pillow.

We found ourselves straining at every sound. But at last we did sleep, although for my part it was a little disjointed. I dreamt I was preparing to appear in a TV show, but I didn't know my part or even which show it was. It was obviously a crime story, because I woke with a jerk having been staring down the barrel of a gun, held by a guy who looked like Robert.

I laughed weakly, and settled down again as well as I could. Then my eyes popped open. There was something in the dream which nagged me. I thought hard. TV crime programme, it rang such a bell.

"Crimewatch" that was it. Then I remembered. In one of the reconstruction scenes, James Staples had played a victim of robbery. Well, that was fair enough, it was his job after all, acting in anything he could get. But no, he hadn't really been acting, he'd been the actual victim and had suffered some injuries.

Why hadn't he mentioned it? Oh dear, I thought. Does this put the couple back on the suspect list?

I woke again to the sound of Pavarotti from the en-suite. Jack sounded as though he hadn't a care in the world. I'd soon put a stop to that, when I told him about James Staples.

Strangely though, Jack was not fazed at all by the news.

"He probably either didn't think it was important, or was a bit embarrassed."

End of story.

Over breakfast we planned our next move. Looking round the dining room, I plumped for the foursome. Jack was unenthusiastic.

"I still think they're harmless yogurt salespeople," he said. "But if your heart's set on it, we'll give it a shot."

Thus, we wandered out of the dining room in their wake. The women seemed to be discussing an establishment which made and sold jewellery and perfume. I was distracted for a few minutes, it did sound rather good.

I had a bright idea. Why not? I asked myself.

"Excuse me," I stepped in quickly, before I changed my mind. I saw Jack looking at me in astonishment.

"I couldn't help overhearing you mention somewhere that sells unusual jewellery." I opened my eyes wide and tried to look innocent.

The women looked at each other then one said, "Yes it's in Bourton-on-the-Water, it really is worth a visit. We go there whenever we're in the area."

"Yes," the other woman said, "this bracelet is one of theirs, isn't it nice? And it didn't cost an arm and a leg. They have a perfumery too, it's absolutely gorgeous."

The bracelet was very pretty indeed.

"It's lovely," I said. "Perhaps we could take a trip there today?" I turned to Jack, making a silent 'no' at him.

He got the message. "Can't do today hon, if you remember I wanted to do a bit of phoning to make sure everything's O.K. back at work. But you go if you like."

I pouted. "It's no fun on my own. I don't think I'll go."

"Come with us," the women said. That's well played Jack, I thought. Just what I wanted.

"Weeel," I said hesitantly, "if you're sure I wouldn't be in the way....."

"No, no," they both assured me. "It'll give us a chance to get to know you."

Ditto, I said to myself.

"We've just got to tidy up a bit, then we could meet back here in about half an hour. I'm Mags, by the way, and this is Jools."

"Pippsy," I said with a smile. "See you in half an hour then."

"What was all that about?" Jack asked when we were back in our room.

"Don't you see, I can grill them and find out for sure who they are and what they do."

Jack shook his head. "You be careful Pips, if they are involved in any funny business, you could be in a heap of trouble. I'm not sure about this, we can't be too careful, not after everything that's happened."

"Oh, I'll be careful," I said beaming at him. He's so lovely when he gets all protective. "I promise I won't take any risks. If I have any doubts, I'll give you a quick ring and say I've just remembered a list of things for you to sort out, or rubbish of that ilk."

So it was, that half an hour later, I was climbing into the back of a very comfortable not to say luxurious BMW.

"A lovely car," I said.

Mags looked smug. "Dave and I change our car every year, plus we like a bit of luxury. Jools and Bill are waiting to take delivery of a new Porsche, which is why we all came in the one car."

So, no shortage of money. But from yogurt? I sat quietly for a while as the car hummed along the roads with scarcely a bump under the wheels.

Jools turned round and asked, "What does your hubby do?"

"He, that is we, have an investigative agency." Well, it sounded better than saying that we were private dicks.

"Ooh," they chorused. "How thrilling, just like those detectives you see in films."

Jools said, "Do you get murder cases and things? I was watching a film the other day, where the detective was trying to find a bloke's girlfriend. Now what was it called? No, can't remember. It was ever so good though."

I had a fair idea which film she meant, but I pretended not to know.

"I'm afraid our cases are not nearly so exciting. It's mostly divorces, or sometimes runaways, or now and again fraud or embezzlement. So, all a bit dull."

By this time we had reached Bourton.

"What do you do?" I asked trying to act casual.

"A bit of this and that," Mags said. "Trading and so forth. Like you, nothing very exciting."

This and that could mean anything, I thought. I was going to have to probe.

"What sort of trading?" I tried innocent again, it usually works.

"We've got a big deal going at the moment," Jools said. I noticed that Mags gave her a warning look.

"But you never know, in business," she finished lamely.

End of that conversation I thought. I'll just have to try again later.

I loved the jewellery and the various trinkets. After some deliberation I treated myself to a pair of earrings. Cornflower design and colour – very pretty. I liked to think they brought out the colour of my eyes.

Mags and Jools had rushes of blood to their heads. They scampered about the shop picking up at least half a dozen pieces each. There was much girlish laughter and comments such as, "Oh no I really shouldn't," or "I think I deserve this – don't you?"

Eventually the spending spree came to an end, and we went to a little coffee shop for a sit down and refreshment.

I carefully – I thought – brought the conversation round to business again. But each time I thought Jools was about to let something slip, Mags chipped in with something that steered the talk onto another subject. It was quite cleverly done, but irritating nevertheless.

We decided to push off back to the hotel after an hour or so. Mags and Jools chattered, seemingly non-stop, about their purchases, where they would go next day and what the 'boys' might have been up to while we were out.

Just once, Jools verged on slipping up. She reminded Mags that they had but two more days, before their deal would be settled. My ears must have pricked up clear of my hair. Once again however, Mags cut her off.

"Pippsy doesn't want to hear about that. It's of no interest whatsoever."

That's what you think, I said to myself.

We reached The Flowerdew around four o'clock. I thanked the ladies for the trip, and said I'd thoroughly enjoyed myself (crossing my fingers behind my back). We went our separate ways. Mags and Jools to show off their purchases no doubt, while I went into the Lounge expecting to see Jack reading the paper and enjoying afternoon tea.

To my surprise there was no sign of him. I peered out of the window, towards the parking bays, but there was no car evident either.

Oh well, I thought, perhaps he's got a couple of leads. With that in mind I made for our room.

The shock I got when I unlocked the door almost stopped my heart.

Our room had been ransacked. Every drawer and cupboard stood open and emptied. Clothes were scattered everywhere, and the bed had been stripped. The en-suite was in complete disarray, our toilet bags turned upside down, a tin of talcum emptied onto the floor, and even tubes of toothpaste and jars of cream emptied.

I stood and looked, totally speechless.

Where was Jack, why wasn't he here? Perhaps he'd spotted whoever was responsible, and gone after them.

I picked up the phone and rang reception. On this occasion, Robert answered, and my heart sank. Nevertheless, I had to tell him what had happened.

There was complete silence at the other end. Oh Gordon, I thought, he's gone again. I said, "Hello, hello," more in despair than anything else.

After a moment a shaky voice responded. He assured me that he would be up instantly, and not to worry, the hotel would pay for any damage or loss.

This last concerned me not at all. I wanted to know who, what and why – and most of all where, in Jack's case.

Robert was as good as his word and was tapping on the door less than five minutes later. His horror when he witnessed the mayhem caused me to fear that he would keel over again. This time however, he managed to stay upright.

He gave a monumental sigh and said, "I suppose I had better ring the police – again." I nodded sympathetically, but at the same time I was aware that I might have some explaining to do – again.

Half an hour later Superintendant Fitzgerald and Sergeant Jones were examining the room.

"Did you touch anything? Anything at all?" the Superintendant barked at me.

"Other than the door handle, not a thing," I said crossly. What did he think I was – an amateur?

"How about the Manager?" The Sergeant asked, peering under the bed.

"Only the phone," I said. "He was much too upset to do anything, other than ring you. He went straight downstairs after that."

"And where is your esteemed husband?" The Super asked. "I would have expected him to be here."

I looked at my watch, it was nearly half five. A vague feeling of panic crept over me. Yes, where was he?

"I don't know where he is. I've been out myself for most of the day. I came back and found this." I hesitated then plunged on, "As a matter of fact, yesterday afternoon when we were having a nap, someone tried to break into the room. I heard the handle being turned and then the sounds of the lock being picked."

The Superintendant's eyebrows almost disappeared into his thinning hair.

"Did it not occur to you to inform us of this?" he enquired.

"Well, actually yes, but then we thought no, because nothing happened. And anyway you had warned us off, so we were trying to keep out of your hair." I knew I was babbling, but I couldn't seem to help it. Where was Jack? If anything had happened to him what would I do?

My face must have showed some of my desperation, because the Superintendant said, "Sit down my dear young lady. I can see you've had a shock. Now, when do you expect your husband to return."

To my and certainly his horror, I burst into tears.

"I don't know, the car's gone, and if he'd been going anywhere important he would have rung my mobile. I know something dreadful's happened to him."

Both the Super and Sergeant tut-tutted, and even patted my back, in the Super's case.

"Now don't go thinking the worst. There's probably some perfectly rational explanation for his not being here, and perhaps your mobile phone was in a no-reception zone when he was trying to ring you."

I howled loudly. "No, he would have gone on ringing, or rung the hotel. Someone's harmed him, I know it. He must have caught them red-handed. They probably killed him and carted his body away."

"Mrs. Standage, pull yourself together. I'm sure that nothing has happened to your husband, you said yourself that the car has gone. He'll come back in time for dinner, with a good reason for his absence." The Super twitched his familiar smile, trying to appear paternal.

I calmed down a little, telling myself the Superintendant was right. Jack was fine. He had to be.

"Now why don't you go downstairs, and order yourself a big drink?"

It sounded reasonable. Anyway, it might settle my nerves, and I could wait for Jack. He'd be furious about the room, but he'd laugh over my exaggerated fears.

I went to the bar, leaving the police to do whatever they needed. If only Jack would ring, just so's I'd know he was alright.

But, he didn't ring, and an hour later after the police had left, I was still sitting in the bar. I could feel panic rising again. In another half an hour it would be dinnertime.

Oh Jack, I thought, my darling where are you?

Robert approached a little tentatively. "Your room has been tidied Mrs. Standage, if you wish to go upstairs. Or if you would prefer, we can move you?"

Poor Robert looked drained of life.

I assured him that our own room was fine, and thanked him for his concern. He looked pathetically grateful, bowed his head and left.

Perhaps I should go upstairs and change or something. It was of no real interest, and the thought of dinner made me decidedly queasy.

Still, more for Robert's benefit than anything, I made my way upstairs. The staff must have worked like demons. Everthing had been hung up or folded away, and even the toothpaste and jars of cream had been replaced.

I had a shower, just to pass the time, but I felt lacklustre and exhausted. I lay on the bed trying to think peaceful thoughts. I must have dozed, because I woke to hear the door being opened very quietly. There wasn't much light, as I'd drawn the curtains before lying down, but there was enough for me to see a shadowy figure come into the room. I made a grab for the table lamp, then jumped off the bed and brandishing the lamp, yelled at the top of my voice, "Don't you try anything, or I'll brain you."

"For crying out loud, Pippsy what's the matter with you. I nearly had a heart attack."

My beloved Jack! I dropped the lamp and threw myself at him. "Where have you been? I thought you were kidnapped or dead. I've been worried sick. I'll never recover from it." With that I burst into tears, again.

"I've been trying to ring you all day. Your phone's out of juice. I rang and left a message at reception a couple of hours ago. It was one of the waiters, I bet the sod didn't bother to tell you did he?"

I shook my head, then through my sobs told him that the room had been ransacked and the police had been called, so I told them how someone had tried to break in..... there I was babbling again. Somehow though, I couldn't have cared less. I was secure in the arms of my beloved, so all was right with the world.

Jack washed his face and hands, and we went down to dinner.

"Well?" I asked.

"What d'you mean 'well'," Jack said.

"Where were you until this time?"

Jack sat munching on a huge steak, his appetite it seemed, restored to its usual gargantuan quality.

"You'll be surprised when I tell you." He went on munching.

"So, tell me!" I just about kept my voice down.

"After you went off with the ladies this morning, I decided to sit in the lounge and read the dailies. I'd just got settled down to the Times crossword..."

"Huh!" I said. Jack never did the Times crossword. Or any other crossword come to think of it.

"Can I tell this in my own way?" he asked. I nodded.

"I saw the husbands making their way out to a taxi. I'm ashamed to say I did a Pippsy. I followed them. I was lucky, because they were having an argument with the taxi driver, which held them up a bit. Anyway, as I said, I followed them. They went to Cheltenham, first to an hotel, then after about an hour – and believe me it was no easy matter parking I can tell you – they went to an office building. Well, while they were inside I had a shufti at the brass plate outside. It was a solicitor. I sat in the car for another hour or so then they came out and went back to the hotel where they began.

"I hung around outside there again, for another hour. I was getting a bit p......d off by this time, but then they came out and made their way back here. So I reckon something's afoot, just don't know what."

He stopped and sat back for a moment, before he began munching again.

I proceeded to tell Jack about my day with the ladies. As I finished we saw the foursome come into the dining room. They had been in the bar, and were obviously feeling no pain.

All four were unsteady on their feet, and made their way to the usual table cautiously. Mags and Jools waved to me and called, "Good day wasn't it Pippsy?"

We ate the rest of our dinner rather silently, thinking how our two stories could mesh. It was back to the bar after dinner, where we tried to make some sense of what each of us had heard and seen.

Presently the foursome reeled in merrily, and made their way over to us.

Robert appeared, to do his usual spot check, but was beckoned over by one of the husbands.

"Come and have a drink, old chap," he said. Robert looked taken aback.

"It wouldn't be proper for me to drink with the guests, sir," he said.

"That's alright old son," he was told. "Guess what? We're your new bosses. We've just bought The Flowerdew, and we'll be taking over from the beginning of next month."

"We've got really big plans for this place," Mags said. "Got to bring it into the 21st Century. Redecorate to start with, get shot of all this country house tat. Modern minimalist is what we're after. It'll be an eye opener, you wait and see."

She turned to Jack and me and said, "We're going to have a couple of bottles of shampoo to celebrate, do join us."

I couldn't look at Jack, and I was sure he couldn't look at me. We nodded and smiled and congratulated the foursome, and hoped they would be very successful.

Robert had brought over two bottles of very expensive champagne, which he proceeded to uncork to much cheering from Mags and Jools.

We enjoyed a glass then excused ourselves and left. I felt that the foursome would be in the bar for some considerable time.

Robert was in reception, talking to Caroline.

I said, "Shall you be staying on Robert? The new owners might like an experienced manager for the first few months at least."

Robert sniffed, "I don't think I would fit in somehow. No, I've a friend in Fulham who wants me to join him in running a little bar. It won't pay so well to begin with, but at least it'll be regular hours, and there's a nice flat to go with it. My nerves can't take much more of this place."

We wished him well, and went upstairs.

"That takes care of that then," I said. "It's not the Fizzy Foursome. So we'll have to keep looking."

“Dead on Arrival
”

“Dead on Arrival
”

Chapter Twenty-Two

In bed that night we talked over our day, and agreed that perhaps we had each been a little precipitate in our efforts.

"Never mind," I said, "we've learned a good lesson. And by the way, I'm not letting you out of my sight for the next hundred years!"

We snuggled down together and promptly fell asleep.

About two o'clock in the morning I awoke to the sound of scratching around the door lock again.

Blow, I thought, we didn't jam the chair against the door. I nudged Jack and whispered, "Someone's trying to get in again."

In a flash he was out of bed, followed by me just marginally more slowly.

He crouched down by the door and grabbed the legs of the bedroom chair.

"You get ready to switch the light on. Any nonsense and I'll clobber them with the chair."

We stayed at the ready for several minutes, until we became aware that the scratching had stopped.

"I'll open the door and you leap out on them," I whispered. As quietly as I could, I turned the key in the lock and eased the door ajar. Jack was poised on the other side, chair at the ready as I flung the door wide. He leapt forward into the corridor, which proved to be empty.

"Where the hell are they?" he asked between gritted teeth.

"How do I know? They realised we were ready for them, and scarpered."

There were emergency lights in the corridor, and Jack prowled up and down a couple of times. "They must have gone down the back stairs, so we haven't got a hope in hell of catching them."

He came back in and prowled up and down the room instead. As we were both wide awake I put the kettle on and made a cup of good old builders tea.

"If it's the room ransackers," I said, "surely they would have realised that we don't have anything. Unless," and I gulped, "they were going to beat the daylights out of us, for information."

Jack pulled his lip. "Could be," he said slowly. "But if that was the case, the fact that we were ready for them wouldn't have mattered. The poor guy in the field received an almighty going over, and he was a heavy, so I can't see them being too worried by the thought of anything we might do."

It made a funny kind of sense. People who were ready to beat up and murder, certainly wouldn't be deterred by the pathetic likes of us.

"No," Jack said, "either they were disturbed, or they've decided to be more devious."

I gulped again.

"We are really going to have to watch our backs, aren't we?" I said faintly.

Jack gave me a squeeze. "I'll watch yours, if you watch mine," he said grinning.

"It's no laughing matter," I said, "we could be in serious danger. I'm ringing the cops first thing in the morning and that's flat."

After our disturbed night, neither of us felt particularly chirpy next morning. Jack tried the first few bars of 'Nessun Dorma', but gave up when he realised how apt the lyric was.

"'None Shall Sleep' is getting to be a habit with us. I'm fed up. Fine holiday this has turned out to be." He looked quite fierce.

"Right," I said, "that's it. Superintendant Fitzgerald here I come." I dialled the number, hoping against hope that the Super was there.

We were in luck, after giving our name to someone who sounded as though they ran three miles before breakfast, the Super came on the line.

He listened to my account of the previous night's shenanigans and said, to my surprise, "I shall be with you in thirty minutes. Don't touch anything whatever you do."

Jack had been listening over my shoulder, and looked as astonished as I felt.

"He took it very seriously, didn't he?" I said.

"It looks to me, as if we're at the sharp end of ....something," Jack said. "We'd better sit tight. I could murder a plate of eggs and bacon. Let's have a cup of tea, and I think there's a few biscuits left in the hospitality drawer, that'll have to do I suppose."

How could he be so interested in his stomach, when all this was happening, I wondered?

We switched on the TV, and sat drinking our tea and nibbling on the biscuits. I think neither of us was concentrating until the announcer said, "The missing businessman Mr. Harry Purvis has been found dead. We have no further details at present, but the police are treating the death as suspicious."

We sat staring at each other. What did it mean, found dead? We'd known he was found dead three days ago, and why was there no mention of Mr. Scarecrow? Or poor old Carmichael, for that matter?

"Well, Pipplet, we've certainly got ourselves smack bang in the middle of something this time."

I had to admit, Jack was very right. In hindsight I wished with all my heart that we'd stayed out of it. But of course, hindsight's a wondrous thing.

As if on cue, there was a firm knock from outside.

I never thought I would say it, but the Super at that moment looked like St. Michael standing there, he only needed the sword.

He must have been taken aback by the effusive welcome I gave him. There was no Sergeant Jones this morning. Probably looking after the police station.

There were two plain clothes men with him, and they immediately began examining the lock, the door, the carpet in the corridor, anything and everything it seemed.

Jack and I perched on the bed, while the Super took over the chaise longue by the window.

"Now," he said, "I suppose I will have to give you a little more information, seeing as you seem to be involved. Unfortunately."

We waited.

"Did you see a news bulletin today? Ah yes, I see that you did. Well, you will have realised that we are releasing certain information, bit by bit I might add, in the hope that those responsible will feel a little – ahem – draught."

We waited.

He appeared to be marshalling his thoughts. Then he leaned forward and looked at us very seriously.

"Mr and Mrs. Standage, your curiosity has got the better of you this time I fancy. I should, in all honesty, take you into custody after all the meddling you have indulged in. And," he held up his hand as I opened my mouth, "I don't want or need any reasons or excuses. I suspect that you thought this case was one of theft and money laundering, with a little murder on the side for good measure. I can tell you, that theft and money laundering are the side issues here. The murders are the tip of the iceberg, as those perpetrating these crimes are not purely home-grown, shall we say. You have unwittingly stumbled into a criminal organisation of world-wide proportions."

I almost fell off the bed. All I could think was "world-wide proportions". I glanced at Jack, he was running a hand through his hair, a sure sign that he was concerned.

The Super had paused significantly, to help us take in what he'd said I presumed. He leaned back into the chaise, steepling his fingers – we're in for the long haul I thought.

"Firstly, let us discuss Mr. Harry Purvis, who had the misfortune to be unable to complete his transactions here at the hotel.

"Mr. Purvis described himself as a businessman. The business in which he engaged however, was funny business. He had been under surveillance for some time, as he had been associating with a small time robber, who had served several terms at Her Majesty's pleasure. He posed as bodyguard to Mr. Purvis, which I believe I told you. Jimmy Cousins as he was called, had a much more important role to play however.

"Mr. Purvis was given a significant sum of money, by a gentleman we shall call Mr. X, which was to be passed to a contact for services rendered. The gentleman who was to receive the money was, as we say, a 'hitman', and had 'hit' two acquaintances of his employer. These gentlemen had apparently, stepped out of line, and although one of them survived, I fear he will not be the man he was.

"We believe that when Mr. Purvis was collecting the hitman's fee, he saw the diamonds, lying around carelessly on this occasion, for their owner is not a careless man. Mr.

Purvis arranged for Cousins to break into Mr. X's home and relieve him of the diamonds. These diamonds would be passed to Mr. Carmichael, for him to dispose of quickly and quietly.

"Alas the best laid plans etc. Mr. Purvis and Mr. Cousins were not quite good enough at thinking their plans through to fruition. As you know, Mr. Cousins met a very unfortunate not to say brutal end.

"Mr. Purvis on the other hand suffered a heart attack. We think, by being threatened by the same treatment as that meted out to Cousins. How the diamonds ended up in the bushes, for you to find, is I suspect, a problem we shall never resolve.

"One can almost feel sorry for Carmichael. He had sailed a little close to the wind once or twice, but for the most part was fairly legit. I suspect the greatest crime he had ever committed, was cheating on his Income Tax, but he was suspected of having squirrelled away both the money and the diamonds.

"Now we all know, that you Mr. and Mrs. Standage, had found the diamonds, and that we, had the money. We can't know just what Carmichael had told his attacker, but we can surmise that you would have figured in there somewhere.

"I fear that you will be viewed with some interest."

I felt the blood drain from my head, and I dropped my head onto my knees. Fainting was not an option, I thought. Jack put his arm round me and held me firmly.

"Honestly Superintendant," he said, "did you have to put things quite so bluntly?"

"Yes, Mr. Standage. I did. If you remember, I warned you on several occasions that you should forget poking into this investigation. As ye sew, so shall ye reap. And while I'm not totally unsympathetic, you must agree that you alone have brought about this state of affairs."

We sat there. Me, starting to shake, and Jack, still holding me firmly.

"Now," he went on, "we shall be providing you with constant protection, but, and I want to stress to you only if you agree, we would like to use you as bait."

My head began swimming again. After everything he'd said, about the danger, and how we'd only got ourselves to blame, he wanted us to put ourselves up as targets. Oh no, no chance, I thought, and waited for Jack to confirm this.

Shock! Horror! Jack said, "If you can guarantee that we'll have round the clock protection, then we're game. We'd like to see it through. Wouldn't we Pippsy?"

"Are you mad? See it through! We'll finish up in our graves. I don't want to do this."

Jack gave me a little shake.

"Oh, alright then, but if we get killed we'll come back and haunt you," I said to the Super.

Chapter Twenty-Three

We finally staggered down to breakfast, and managed – well I managed – tea and toast. Jack of course, had his usual full English.

The Super had given us a run down on how we should play things.

He suggested we should continue talking to the other guests.

"We're pretty sure," he said, "that there are one or two suspects still hanging around. It explains the ransacking of your room, plus the attempted break-ins."

At all costs, he stressed, we must appear carefree. "Keep any conversations on a trivial level," he told us. "Talk about shopping, Mrs. Standage. The latest cricket score or something, Mr. Standage. Don't mention the murders, and try and make a joke of the break-in should you be asked."

Having been thus briefed, the Super appeared satisfied with us.

"Remember, there'll be one or two of our men around at all times. Should an emergency arise, here's my mobile number. I trust that you won't need it, and that we shall soon be bringing the case to a satisfactory conclusion."

With that we had to be content. But the first thing that entered my mind was, we wouldn't be cutting back on our alcohol consumption for a while.

"I wonder where the Super's men are?" I said, as we left the dining room.

"Probably skulking in the bushes, or hiding in cupboards," Jack replied. "Don't worry Pippsy, it'll be OK you'll see, and think how good it'll look, the next time we need to approach the police for help with a case."

I was unconvinced. I wanted to see good old uniformed bobbies, patrolling the place.

"What shall we do today?" Jack asked. "D'you fancy a run out somewhere. I mean if we're supposed to be on holiday, it would look natural wouldn't it?"

I supposed so, but for the life of me I couldn't fancy trawling round the Cheltenham shops.

"Let's just get in the car and drive," I said.

We set out about an hour later, stopping for petrol on the way, and looking at some of the leaflets I'd collected.

"There's an interesting museum mentioned," Jack said. "Musical boxes etc. How about that?"

"If you like." I honestly couldn't get steamed up about anything.

The sky was overcast, so perhaps somewhere undercover was a good idea. As we drove along, I gradually became more relaxed.

"This was a good idea," I said. "I feel much better now."

We put the radio on, and sang along to a couple of old sixties favourites. Even the clouds cleared a bit. I felt almost cheerful.

"Shall we stop somewhere for coffee?" Jack was thinking about the inner man. Again.

We found a twee little coffee shop in one of the villages. It was actually quite pretty, just a bit overdone. Still, the coffee was good, and I stretched a point and had a large slice of a scrumptious looking cake.

As we were paying the bill, I peered out of the window, to see what the weather was doing. It had got a bit cloudy again. There was a car parked opposite, which drove off quickly as we emerged. I could have been mistaken, although I didn't think so. It looked just like the honeymooners.

"Did you notice that car?" I asked.

"Which car?" Jack said.

"The one that just drove away. It was parked across the street."

"No, can't say I did. Why?"

"It was the honeymooners, I'm sure it was."

"Why would they drive off then, you would have thought they'd have stopped to say 'hello'?"

I was puzzled, then a bit worried. "Do you think they were following us?"

"Now why would they be following us? If it was them, it's pure coincidence. They probably drove off because they were embarrassed." It made sense. All the same I couldn't shake the feeling that something was not right.

"D'you think they could be a couple of the Super's officers?" I said.

"Rubbish," Jack answered. "If they were the law, they wouldn't be honeymooners, would they?"

We got into the car and continued on our way. For me though, it was a little niggly problem, that wouldn't go away.

The threatened rain materialised. A light drizzle to begin with, then suddenly the heavens opened and water cascaded down the windscreen. The wipers couldn't cope.

"I'm going to pull over and park," Jack said. "It's sure to ease off in a few minutes."

We were in a country lane, with high hedges, but we pulled over anyway. Except we didn't stop. Jack was thumping the brake. His face was white.

"The bloody brake's not working," he said. Luckily we were on a level stretch, but country lanes have a nasty habit of having sharp bends, or sloping away, when you least expect it.

My mouth had gone dry, and I could see Jack's jaw twitching as he clenched his teeth.

"Try the handbrake," I suggested. That was useless, and sure enough the ground began to slope away as we rounded a bend.

Jack turned off the ignition and steered us into the nearest hedge. It was a rough contact, but thankfully there was no ditch. We stopped. I found I'd been holding my breath, and I took a great gasp of air, which developed into a fit of coughing.

“My God, I thought that was it,” Jack said, breathing hard.

“What on earth happened to the brakes?” I said. “They were fine when we set out. It was only after we'd stopped for..for..” I horrible thought had struck me.

“The car parked opposite to the cafe. The one I said had the honeymooners in it. Do you think it's possible, that they tampered with the brakes, while we were having coffee?”

Jack looked at me as though I'd taken leave of my senses.

“Pippsy, I can't believe you just said that. I'm sure there's some logical, if terrifying, solution. Anyway, I'm going to ring the AA and get this sorted out.”

The AA arrived about half an hour later. The mechanic jacked the car up and checked underneath. When he emerged, his face was pale.

“These brakes have been cut,” he said. “Someone's got it in for you. I think we'd better call the police.”

We rang the Super's mobile.

In a slightly shaky voice, I told him what had happened.

“Stay where you are, I'll be there very shortly. You were supposed to be followed wherever you went, I'll have somebody's hide for this.” There was cold fury in his voice.

I didn't envy the officer or officers who were supposed to be protecting us. Not one little bit.

Chapter Twenty-Four

The Super arrived very quickly. There were two shame-faced plain clothes officers with him. They explained that their car had been disabled at the hotel. By the time they had arranged for a replacement, we were long gone.

Naturally enough, my suggestion that the disabling of the brakes took place while we were enjoying coffee, was dismissed instantly. It would have been impossible, I was told, for the brakes to have been cut by the roadside.

"It is likely," the Super said, "that any tampering took place at the hotel. Probably during the night. Whoever did this would have been careful to make sure that the brakes would fail after a few miles. Which of course, is just what occurred. Thankfully, you were not in a particularly dangerous situation. Nevertheless, it must have been quite unsettling for you."

We were, by this time, comfortably established in the bar at the hotel – where else? Enjoying medicinal glasses of brandy. All the same, I felt that the words 'quite unsettling' was something of an understatement.

"I think," the Super continued, "that we had better arrange much closer protection for you. It does appear, that these people are definitely concerned about your involvement. Having dangled you in front of them, they've snapped at the bait. You do not, of course, have to continue with this plan. No one would think any less of you, if you opted to walk away. I would remind you however, that the people of whom we speak, will most likely have a dossier on you, and should you decide to return home, it would be more difficult to keep you under our wing."

Jack took my hand. "If Pippsy wants to leave, then that's what we'll do."

Everyone looked at me enquiringly.

I opened my mouth to say that I wanted to go home, and never be a Private Investigator again, instead I found myself saying stoutly, "Nobody's going to chase me away. Jack and I are going to stay with it, and bring these people to book. So there!"

I can't imagine why I added that last childish phrase, but it seemed to go down well. The Super, his officers and Jack, all beamed at me, as if I'd solved the case singlehandedly.

The next problem of course was sorting out a replacement car, and informing our Insurers of our misfortune. The agent to whom we spoke was suitably shocked and sympathetic, and as the police had removed the car for forensic examination, assured us that our policy was in no way compromised.

By the sound of it, our predicament was far more interesting than the problems with which she normally dealt.

We mooched around for the rest of the day, and at about five o'clock our replacement car arrived. I definitely felt better once we had wheels again, although I couldn't for the life of me think why!

Our guardian angels, PC's Perkins and Hawkesley, were very discreet. Neither of them was in any way extraordinary. In fact, PC Perkins with his gelled hair and baby face, reminded me of a sixth form schoolboy. Hawkesley had a slightly thuggish air, shaven head and all. One wouldn't have given them a second look under normal circumstances. Except of course, these were not normal circumstances.

Trying to appear casual, I asked Perkins, why he had joined the police. He shrugged and said his A level results had not been good enough for anything else.

Next, I asked Hawkesley his reasons for joining the Force. He too shrugged, and said it was better than his previous job, as a nightclub bouncer!

After that I rather gave up. Still, I thought, a bouncer should be able to handle anything threatening.

After dinner, we retired to our room. I had looked carefully round the dining room but there were not many eating in, it seemed. The family were obviously leaving next day. I heard the father asking for an early call.

There was no sign of the foursome, and Mr. Jankowsky requested a plate of sandwiches at the bar.

The honeymooners put in a brief appearance, so I watched them closely. They appeared to have eyes for no one but each other, and finished their meal with great speed, before disappearing upstairs in some haste. Jack gave me a long look.

"Still think that they're suspicious?"

I sighed, "I don't know who's suspicious and who isn't anymore. Everything's such a muddle. Let's have an early night, I'm worn out."

We nodded to our minders, and went up for what I fervently hoped would at last, be a good night's sleep.

I decided on a soak in the bath, and Jack plumped for a malt and an hour of "Law and Order". When we finally settled down, I felt more relaxed than I had for a while.

There was, alas, just that slight uneasiness, because we hadn't yet had closure to the whole affair.

The bath and "Law and Order" obviously did the trick, as we both slept like logs. In fact I awoke next morning laughing. I had been having some ludicrous dream or other.

Jack rolled onto his back and stretched.

"You sound jolly, Pips. Feeling more like your old self?"

"We both had a decent night for once," I told him, smiling. "Maybe they've realised we don't know anything, and have given up on us?"

"I wouldn't count on it. There's more to come I fear, but at least if we're rested we'll be better equipped."

I admitted that he was probably right.

Presently, 'Nessun Dorma' rang out vibrantly.

Our guardians approached us unobtrusively after breakfast, querying our plans for the day.

"We could have a second try at that museum?" Jack said.

I hesitated, unsure whether I wanted to travel the same route again. But then I thought that lightening surely wouldn't strike twice – so why not?

We set out very cautiously. Jack tried the brakes every few minutes, and must have been a source of great irritation to the drivers behind us. We had chosen a slightly different route as we had no wish to use the same road as the previous day.

Perkins and Hawkesley shadowed us, a discreet distance behind. I began to enjoy the drive, and looked forward to a nice day out.

The museum proved to be enchanting, and I almost maxed out my credit card, selecting gifts in the shop.

Jack, although a little more restrained, bought me a lovely little music box, which played "Love me tender". I'm no great fan of Elvis, but this sounded so charming that I fell in love with it.

At dinner that evening however, I began to feel uneasy again. I couldn't shake off the feeling that someone other than our guardians, was watching us. Jack shrugged when I told him.

"What d'you expect?" he said. "This performance has been going on practically from day one. Just stay loose, act natural and look as though you're enjoying yourself. If we are being watched, we want them to think we haven't a care in the world."

We took our coffee in the bar, and I looked around me as naturally as I could. All the usual suspects were present, the Barnsworths, Mr. Jankowsky and his girlfriend, the foursome, plus a sprinkling of new arrivals. There was no sign of the honeymooners, so I wondered if they'd left.

Our guardians were relaxing in the lounge, sipping coffee and mineral water. I guessed they would have enjoyed something a little stronger, but of course, they were on duty.

At last Jack decided to call it a night. As we passed through the lounge on our way upstairs, I caught the eye of Perkins, or maybe it was Hawkesley, I could never remember which was which. To my astonishment, he winked and pursed his lips knowingly. I felt myself turn pink. I had a fair idea what he meant.

Fat chance, I thought. With what we've been through the last few days, sleep is the only thing we're interested in.

Still, it took me some time to drop off. I was listening for suspicious noises then wondering why I couldn't hear any, and twice I crept out of bed and put my ear to the door.

Jack, of course, was blissfully unaware of anything. Which was his usual mode.

I asked him once how he was able to sleep, no matter what problems assailed us. He said it was the sleep of the innocent. I recall I punched him. Hard!

We awoke safe and sound next morning. Jack in fact, leapt out of bed like a greyhound out of the traps, and even "Nessun Dorma" was not unpleasing to my ears.

Perhaps everything will just go away, I said to myself as I showered. Perhaps we can have a day free from care. Perhaps we can complete our romantic break in the proper style.

I was reminded of an old song, and hummed "Perhaps, perhaps, perhaps".

"What shall we do today?" I asked my beloved, who was examining his hairline with a worried expression.

"D'you know Pippsy," he said, "I think my hair's starting to recede. What do you think?" he turned to look at me.

I opened my mouth to say, "Don't be such a plonker," or some such, when there was a tapping at the door.

Jack crossed the room, and unlocked the door. Before he could open it, it was thrust at him with such force that he staggered back and almost fell.

Standing in the doorway were the honeymooners, the man brandishing a small, nasty looking gun. "Get your clothes on if you please, Mrs. Standage," the woman said with a smile.

"Wha..what's going on?" I croaked.

"I think you know very well. Both of you." The man had an ugly twist to his mouth.

"What do you think you're doing?" Jack tried indignation.

The man gave what I can only describe as a nasty snigger. I felt my heart drop into my feet. Oh lord, I thought, where are Perkins and Hawkesley? Why aren't they here?

"If you're wondering where your guardian angels are?" the woman said, "I'm afraid they're not with us."

"What have you done to them?" I squeaked, thinking, my God they're dead.

"Nothing that need concern you," the man answered. "Now then, when we walk downstairs, we're going to look very casual and friendly – you're quite good at that aren't you? Then we'll stroll out to the car - I'm afraid there won't be time for breakfast today, and then we're all going for a nice little drive."

"Where are we going?" I could hear the shake in my voice, but thought, don't appear to be frightened.

"There is someone who would very much like to talk to you," the woman said. "There's going to be lots to talk about, so I should prepare yourselves for a long day."

She and the man exchanged glances then they both laughed.

It was not pleasant.

Chapter Twenty-Five

We tried very hard to look comfortable as we walked through the foyer. Robert was on his own. He looked up and wished us 'Good morning'. I had a crazy notion that perhaps we could give him some sort of signal that all was not well, but our captors stepped in very close.

"Don't get any ideas Mrs. Standage," the man murmured. "You wouldn't want anything unpleasant to happen, would you?"

I smiled weakly and kept walking, but how I wished Robert would notice that something was not quite right.

Once in our captors car I felt my stomach turn over. What were we to do? We had no recourse now. The Super would never know what had happened to us, even if Perkins and Hawkesley were still in the land of the living. Which I doubted.

Jack was in the front next to the man, while I was kept under close scrutiny by the woman. I wondered what she was thinking. Presently she leaned towards me and said, "You could do with watching your weight. You're not too bad at the moment, but you'll run to fat when you get older if you're not careful."

Despite our predicament, I felt a burst of fury. I was about to retort, then it occurred to me that at least she intimated that I would get older.

We were travelling at a fair old lick, and if nothing else good could be said about him the driver was certainly very expert.

After about half an hour we swung through the gates of a very stately-looking home. Had our position not been so dire, I would have been thrilled to think we were going to be privileged enough to see inside.

The road had been climbing for some way, and the house appeared to be built into the side of the hill. It reminded me of the house in "North by Northwest".

We were urged, rather than ushered, inside.

As one would expect, an imposing panelled entrance hall, walls lined with oil paintings of course, and a number of leather chairs scattered about. We didn't have time for sightseeing however. The man knocked at a pair of handsome carved wood doors and waved the gun for us to enter.

They didn't speak, not even to say, "Here they are."

The room was vast, sofas, chairs and tables abounded, and obviously priceless rugs, were scattered on the beautiful parquet floor.

In front of a magnificent marble fireplace stood a man. His back was turned. We walked the length of the room.

I was shocked when he swung round and revealed himself as Mags's husband, Dave.

"Well, well, well, Mr. and Mrs. Standage. 'Four Eyes Everywhere'. Such a pity you didn't choose to keep those eyes for each other. You really shouldn't go poking into other people's business. It's unhealthy. Not to say dangerous."

Dave eyed us up and down. I could feel my knees beginning to shake, and reached out for Jack's hand.

"We didn't mean to cause problems, it was a pure accident," I managed to say. "We'd come to The Flowerdew for a romantic break, then everything happened so suddenly. But we don't know anything, or want to know anything. We just want to finish our holiday?" I ended on a hopeful upward note.

His eyes bored into me.

"Mrs. Standage, your ceaseless chatter is a bore. I suggest you say nothing more, and try listening instead."

Jack squeezed my hand. I stood there looking back at this man, so well dressed, posing as a legitimate businessman, but instead a criminal and probably a murderer.

What came over me I shall never know. I heard myself saying, "Don't you dare tell me what to do. My husband and I are totally innocent of any criminal activity whatsoever, we've been caught up in something of which we have no knowledge, and little interest. We were brought here against our will at gunpoint, and all we want is to finish our holiday, then return home to continue our business. You may think you are at the top of your game, and maybe you are, but it's of no consequence to us. Now, I demand that you return us to our hotel - which of course is now your hotel, so that we may pack up and leave."

The man's jaw had dropped, ever so slightly. Then to my astonishment, he burst out laughing.

"Mrs. Standage," he said, "you are one feisty lady. I like that, I like it a lot, but you must see that I can't just let you and your husband go back home. You know far too much, and I know you're extremely palsy with a certain Superintendant, who was posing as something rather less at one stage. I shall be reluctant to dispose of such a gutsy couple as yourselves. Leave it with me. You must remain here as my guests, while I think things over."

He nodded to the couple in the doorway, who came and escorted us out of the room.

We were led upstairs to a handsome room, with a magnificent super king size bed. In any other scenario, I would have been agog, but somehow the charm of the surroundings left me cold.

Our captors had closed and locked the door of course, but it didn't deter Jack from examining it carefully, and fiddling with the handle a few times.

"I don't think, somehow," he said, "that we shall be going anywhere. The door is a couple of inches thick. Built to withstand any attempts to force it open."

I agreed, but I couldn't speak. My throat felt as though it had closed up completely.

"That was a fine speech you made downstairs," Jack went on. "Despite everything, I got a feeling that Mr. X, if that's who he is, was quite impressed. He's probably used to women fainting away when they're in such a situation."

My legs began to shake again, as I thought of other people who might have been faced with the kind of threat we had received.

"What d'you think he's going to do," I whispered. "Are we really going to end up on adjacent slabs in the mortuary. Oh dear lord, there must be something we can do."

Jack took me in his arms, and I put my head on his shoulder.

"We've got to play along for a while. Mr. X said he was going to think. I've got a bit of an idea, but be assured Pippsy, we're not going down without a fight. We've been in tightish corners before - not as tight as this I admit - but we always came out on top. It's going to be the same this time, you wait and see."

I felt slightly comforted. Jack is a very strong, logical man, and if he said we'd come out on top, then we very well might.

The sound of the door being unlocked pulled us apart.

It opened slowly and an elderly man pushing a trolley laden with several dishes with silver covers, a coffee pot, cups, plates and cutlery, tottered into the room.

"Good morning, sir – madam," he said. "The master thought you might care for some breakfast? I understand you missed yours."

I opened my mouth to tell him to get lost, but Jack leapt in and with a smile said, "That would be very much appreciated. Thank him for us will you ..er....er.....what was your name?"

"Jeavons, sir. I shall be sure and tell the master that you were very grateful." He almost bowed his way out, but the door was firmly closed and locked again.

Jack was exploring the trolley's bounty.

"Cor' look at this lot," he said. "Kidneys, sausages, eggs, bacon, mushrooms and if I'm not mistaken, black pudding. What a feast, let's get stuck in."

"How can you possibly consider food at a time like this?" I screeched. "We could be face to face with eternity at any moment, and you're thinking about your stomach!"

"Got to keep our strength up," Jack said, helping himself to a plateful. "You should eat something Pippsy, I don't want you swooning from hunger, if effort and quick thinking are required."

Despite myself I found the look of the food very appetising. "I'll just have a bite or two of something," I said.

We sat down at a table in the window, and proceeded to eat. To my surprise, I found I was hungry.

As we were by the window, I looked out from time to time, between mouthfuls. Presently, the honeymooners, as I still thought of them, appeared and made their way to their car.

"Look, Jack," I said excitedly, "the honeymoon couple seem to be on their way."

Jack looked up. "Perhaps their job's done now that we're under wraps. Still it does put a slightly different complexion on things. I wonder if he's got anymore heavies stashed away in the house?"

The couple outside were standing by the car talking. She seemed to be remonstrating with him. Anyway, there was much arm waving going on.

For his part, he was looking around as if she wasn't there. After a few more minutes of this they both climbed in, and drove away.

"Don't look quite so lovey-dovey now, do they?" I said. "I bet they're not on their honeymoon. Probably not even married. Still I would've liked to hear what she was going on about. Wish my lip reading was better, or we'd been closer. Perhaps I'll take a course, after we get...." I stopped.

Jack didn't seem to be listening. He'd finished eating, and was looking carefully at the cutlery.

"It's a funny thing you know," he said, "they've given us what could be lethal weapons. I can't help thinking there's a lot more going on than we could even imagine!"

Chapter Twenty-Six

We finished our breakfast, and I did feel a tad better.

Jack prowled around the room, opening and closing cupboard doors, and pulling aside the curtains at the huge window.

"What on earth are you doing?" I said. "Why don't you sit down and think about our situation?"

"That, my little crumpet is just what I am doing." Jack had a far-away expression on his face.

"I'm wondering," he said, "if there are any secret panels in here. The house is certainly an innovative design. Just the sort of place that might have hidey-holes."

"Coo-er," I jumped up. "Why didn't I think of that. You clever old hubby you."

"Don't get too excited, there might not be any, but all the same, it's worth exploring."

I joined in with alacrity, at least it was something to do, and kept my mind off darker thoughts.

We must have poked and tapped for about twenty minutes, all to no avail. What a disappointment! We collapsed onto the bed, just as the door was unlocked, and Jeavons tottered in to remove the trolley.

"Was there anything else sir and madam would like?"

"Just to get out of here," I snapped.

He nodded his head, and backed out pulling the trolley.

"We should have pounced on him," I said. "A man of his years couldn't possibly have fought us off."

"Don't be too sure," Jack said. "I thought I detected a slight bulge under one of his arms. He could have been carrying."

"Oh no," I was horrified. What other revelations would there be before the day was out? We should last that long, I thought!

I jumped off the bed and began pacing to and fro. Something was niggling me. What had sparked it off? I paced backwards and forwards.

For such an eye catching, imposing house, the floorboards were very creaky. Every other step I took seemed to produce a sound like a groan.

That was it! The floor!

"Jack," I said quietly. "What if there's something under the floor? A trapdoor of some sort?"

He stopped pulling his lip, and climbed off the bed.

"What gave you that idea?"

"These creaks and groans from the floor. It sounds more than normal floorboards would produce."

"Right, let's be systematic. We'll start over by the window, and gradually roll back the rug."

We knelt and began rolling the rug, a huge, heavy Persian jobbie. Eventually we reached the bed, but there was no way we were going to be able to lift it. We sat back on our heels and viewed the situation.

"Let's try from the other side," I said.

Once again we knelt and started rolling.

Still nothing. I felt deflated, it had seemed such a good idea. We rolled the carpet back into place.

Jack stood up and walked to the door.

"Bear in mind," he said, "that anyone wanting to use a trapdoor, wouldn't want to be moving furniture or carpets around. Let me think."

He began walking round the room, close to the wall. Every so often he stamped his foot, then just as he reached the corner - "Bingo!" he murmured.

There was a small table with a long tablecloth draped over it. He lifted it carefully to one side, and bent down.

"Over here Pipps," he said. I walked over and bent to look.

There was a faint but definite change in the lay of the floorboards. We knelt and started running our hands over the floor.

Then at last, "Got it!" Jack said.

It looked like a knot in the wood, but when Jack pressed it there was a click and a section of the boards lowered itself and slid to one side.

We peered into the cavity. It was easily big enough for a body to pass through. The only problem was, it was too dark to see what you were passing into!

"If only we had a torch," I fumed. "In films the leading characters always have matches, or cigarette lighters."

But Jack was sitting on the edge of the opening feeling around with his feet.

"There's a step or something. I'm sure of it," he said.

"Be careful for goodness sake," I hissed. We were both practically whispering, whether through nerves or caution there was no telling.

He put a hand on either side of the opening and began lowering himself into the void.

"There's a staircase here," he said, "and – yes a handrail. I'm going down."

"Not without me you're not," I gulped.

"I'm just going for a reccie. You stay where you are in case anyone comes. Be ready to cover the trapdoor."

I yelped a bit, but I could see the sense of what he was saying.

As Jack disappeared I looked around to see if I could spot any kind of light that I could use. I was petrified in case I heard a yell and a thump. The only vaguely useful thing was a lamp on the table we had moved.

I switched it on and held it over the opening. Jack was right, there was a well-constructed staircase, with a sturdy handrail. Better still though was a switch just beside the top step. I pressed it, and the whole place lit up.

"Oy," Jack called, "how did you manage that?" I smirked, pity he wasn't there to see it.

"Used the old brainpower," I said.

Then I had a thought. Anyone wanting to make a getaway would have to have a way of shutting the trapdoor, to foil pursuers.

I groped under the stairs, but there was nothing other than dirt and cobwebs. Perhaps the underside of the knot Jack had pressed was the key.

I lowered myself very cautiously onto the stairs. Once my head was below the level of the floor, I ran my hand over the trapdoor. Sure enough, there was a matching knot. Now, should I press it or not? If I pressed it would we be able to get out again? And just as importantly what went on at the bottom of the stairs?

So many questions, and no certainty about any answers.

"I think I've found a way out," Jack called. "Hang on and I'll come back."

"Don't worry," I called back, "I'm coming down. I think I've found a way to shut the trapdoor too, but I want to cover our tracks as much as possible."

I lifted myself onto the edge, and managed to manoevre the table over me. Then I lowered myself onto the stairs again.

I pressed the knot, and the door slid across and lifted itself into position.

We met up at the bottom of the stairs.

"That door is kept well oiled, because it doesn't make a sound," I said. "I wonder how many times it's in use?"

We looked at each other. Myriad ideas running through my head. Disposal of bodies, or kilos of heroin, or maybe sackloads of dosh. The possibilities were endless, and one mustn't forget the diamonds!

We tip-toed along a passageway, which was just high enough for Jack to stand upright. The walls, when my hand brushed against one, felt damp and powdery. I guessed we were into the hillside now. The further we progressed, the darker it became of course. I started to feel a bit claustrophobic. Was it my imagination, or were the walls drawing closer together? I swallowed hard, and grabbed Jack's hand.

"Not much further I think," he said. "I can feel a draught of air from up ahead."

Thanks be, I thought. I've never been too keen on enclosed spaces, but this was something else!

As we plodded on, I could feel the air too, but we could hear something now. There was a throbbing sound, as if a muffled engine was running.

Now what, I thought? I began to feel this wasn't such a good idea.

There was a faint glimmer of light ahead. We slowed down, and crept along, feeling for each step that we took.

The light grew brighter, and we could hear voices, even the odd burst of laughter.

The passage turned sharply to the left, and Jack stopped so suddenly that I ran into his back. He turned and put his finger to his lips. I peered over his shoulder as best I could and nearly dropped in my tracks.

Luckily we were shielded, because below us was a huge cavern with enormous arc lights illuminating the scene. The place had been hewn out of the hillside. On the ledge in front of us, was an iron ladder leading down to the floor.

There must have been a dozen or so men in there, tending several gigantic machines. They moved about quickly and efficiently, feeding large sheets of paper in, and checking as the paper moved out further down the line.

It looked like a scene from a film about newspaper printing...... then it hit me so hard I almost squeaked out loud. It wasn't newspapers that were being printed. It was money! We'd stumbled into what looked like a counterfeiting operation.

Chapter Twenty-Seven

We stood, holding onto each other for dear life.

In other circumstance, I would have been fascinated by the procedures I was watching. Sheet after sheet of banknotes, which eventually disappeared into crates, obviously ready for distribution to.......well, somewhere.

I peered at the crates as hard as I could, trying to read the printing on the sides. When I finally deciphered the lettering, I gave a gasp and almost laughed. The destination was not visible, but what I did see on each crate was, '24 boxes, yogurt – mixed flavours'.

Jack turned to look at me, and I whispered, "Yogurt, mixed flavours. I wasn't that wrong after all, was I?"

Jack shook his head. "You have the luck of the Irish sometimes, but that's about to run out, if we can't find some way of getting out of here. For all we know our disappearance may have been discovered, and several unpleasant people could be making their way along the tunnel, even as we speak."

He was right of course.

"Let's backtrack," I said. "There may be another way out that we missed."

We began retracing our steps. Groping along the walls, we hoped we might find another tunnel branching off.

It looked as though we were out of luck. As the light on the staircase gradually appeared I was convinced that the only way out, would be the way we came in.

Then my hand touched what felt like a knob. I pulled Jack's hand and said, "I think I've found something."

We felt the wall carefully, until we located the knob again.

Jack pushed it firmly then pulled it, equally firmly several times. Nothing happened.

"Try twisting it," I said. He twisted left and right. Still nothing.

So, I grabbed the knob, pushed and twisted it to the right. There was a slight creaking sound, and part of the rock wall swung inwards.

"Yes!" I punched the air with excitement.

"Hang on, hang on," Jack said. "In the first place, it might not lead anywhere, and in the second place, which should be the first place, we might get in there, and not be able to get out again."

The thought of being shut into a dark hole with no way out, made me shiver. Still we had to do something.

"Why don't I go in and have a look? You can stand out here and hold the door open." I thought this was very brave of me.

"Are you going completely lala?" Jack said. "You're useless when you can't see your way around. No, if anyone's going in there, it's going to be me."

Right again, Jack.

"If for any reason the door closes – I mean it could be automatic for all we know – I'll open it again straight away." I sounded more positive than I felt.

Jack patted my head. Usually I would have given him a kick, but today it felt very comforting.

"Back in a jiffy," he said, and disappeared through the doorway.

He seemed to be gone for hours, although it was probably only a few minutes before he put his head out.

"Come on Pippsy," he said. "There's what looks like a doorway along here. But we'll have to try and close this one once we get inside."

I didn't like the sound of that, but I couldn't think of any other solution.

I stepped through, and felt for a knob of some sort on the other side of the door. Luckily there was one, and with a pull and a turn the door creaked closed.

Standing there in the dark, I became aware of a faint glow.

"What's that light?" I asked.

"The rock further up has been painted, I think. Some sort of luminous paint. Follow me." Which I did, the tooter the sweeter.

We came up to a door constructed of steel.

It was bolted top and bottom, but there didn't seem to be any lock. The handle was an iron ring. We stood there, just looking at it.

"Well, are we going to open it or what?" I said.

"Guess so," was the reply.

Taking deep breaths we undid the bolts. Then several even deeper breaths, and Jack carefully turned the handle. For a minute I thought the door wasn't going to budge, but it did, and the sweet smell of fresh air and blessed daylight was upon us.

We emerged into shrubbery. The door had been set into the hillside and shrubs concealed the entrance from a mainish road. We stumbled out as fast as we could, and stood for a few minutes gulping the air and trying to decide which way to go.

It didn't seem to matter, so we set off fast, ready to dive off into the bushes, if there were any signs of traffic.

We must have been walking for half an hour or so, when we spotted chimneys and a roof behind a hedge.

"Now what do we do?" Jack said. "The house could belong to the estate, or someone quite innnocent. What do you want to do? Keep going, or chance a knock at the door?"

I chewed a fingernail. "Oh lord, I don't know," I said. "Half of me says knock at the door, the other half says run like hell."

"Let's just wander past and look the place over," Jack said finally. "If anyone's looking out of the window, they might think we're holidaymakers."

Trying to look as though we took country walks as a matter of course, we strode along. The house proved to be a red brick cottage, with small leaded light windows.

There was a gate between high hedges, with a paved path leading to a sturdy-looking wood front door. The front garden was very pretty, a mass of Spring flowers and small shrubs.

It was the sort of house in which I could picture us growing old.

“Let's chance it,” I said. “If some thuggish looking bloke opens the door, we'll just have to run for our lives.”

More deep breaths. We opened the gate and walked up the path. There was a brass doorknocker in the shape of a smiley face, so we knocked.

After a few minutes the door was opened by a young woman with a baby on her hip.

The baby grinned at me, and I instinctively grinned back. I'm a sucker for babies.

“May I help you?” She had a smiley face.

Jack chucked the baby under the chin (he's a sucker too) and said, “What a cutee. Er.. sorry to bother you, our car ran out of petrol a way back, could we possibly use your phone?”

“Of course,” smiling even more, she swung the door open. Somewhere in the back of my head an alarm bell rang. Her face was vaguely familiar.

I had it. The honeymoon woman, this one was very like her. I gave Jack a sharp poke. "I've just had a thought," I said quickly, "we ought to go back to the car, I didn't lock it up, and all your er..er.. fishing tackle is in the boot. Would you excuse us? We'll be back in a sec."

Jack's mouth had dropped open, but he's learned to pick up quickly.

"Yes, dammit, you're right sweetheart." The 'sweetheart' is our own code for, 'you take the lead I'll follow'.

We positively ran down the path, waving over our shoulders, and saying "back in a few minutes, sorry about this."

When we reached the road, Jack turned to me and said, "What was all that about?"

"That woman, she was a dead ringer for the honeymoon woman. Could be a sister or something. Anyway, I thought she was a mite too friendly to two strangers. Just a feeling I had."

Jack gave me a squeeze, "I trust your instincts Pipps. We'd better get a move on in case she's ringing someone we might not want to meet."

Chapter Twenty-Eight

We took a fast pace, putting as much distance as we could between ourselves and the house. My nerves were all a-jangle, which of course accounted for my shortness of breath, rather than the fact I was less than fit.

Jack loped along easily, as if he did this sort of thing every day. However, he glanced over his shoulder once or twice. There were no signs of pursuit that we could see, although we got a bit twitchy when we heard the sound of a motor in the distance.

At last we saw a sign welcoming us to Little Hoo.

Thankfully, one of the first buildings proved to be the Police station. It was an old place, resembling a private house, which it probably had been once upon a time.

The young officer at the desk, praise be, was very much on the ball. We explained who we were and asked if we could borrow the phone to ring Superintendant Fitzgerald.

From there it was all action. I suspected that the young P.C., whose name was Boot (how perfect was that), had never known such excitement. His boyish face became flushed and his eyes sparkled. Probably the biggest crime Little Hoo had ever had, was when the village drunk (there was always a village drunk), forgot himself and p....d in the churchyard up against a gravestone.

The Super sounded very relieved when we finally spoke to him. It seemed Perkins and Hawkesley had not gone to the big CID room in the sky. They had drunk their morning coffee then keeled over. When Robert had discovered them he joined them in no time flat.

The coffee dregs were at present being analysed, but it was fairly certain that some powerful narcotic and been introduced.

I admit, I sighed with relief. I'd grown quite fond of our guardians, even if so far they had been totally useless. There was still time for them to prove themselves, but I wasn't holding my breath.

The Super suggested that we stay put, in the safe hands of the law. We supposed we were in the safest place, unless Dave and his henchmen burst in waving guns about. I couldn't quite see P.C. Boot throwing himself in front of us as a shield!

We were treated to atrocious cups of coffee, which we accepted with a smile, then looked around for a dumping spot. There was a sickly looking plant in one corner, which was the recipient, probably not for the first time.

Eventually, with roaring of engines and screeching of tyres the Super and his backup arrived.

I thought P.C. Boot was going to swoon at the Super's feet. He would be reliving this for the next ten years at least, I felt sure.

After a few minutes we settled in a rather uncomfortable interview room, and got to grips with our adventures so far.

The Super listened without speaking, until we came to the end.

"You have been a very resourceful young couple," he said. "I can tell you that the information you have gathered is very useful to our operation. The fact that your lives have been at risk, makes your actions all the more commendable."

Jack and I sat basking in all the praise and valediction. I felt myself swelling with pride. It hasn't all been for nothing, I told myself. We've proved ourselves, over and above the call.

I came crashing down to earth as the Super continued.

"Nevertheless, you have been both foolish and reckless. From nothing more than pure luck you have come through unharmed. When you return to your normal life, I shall make it my business to apprise your local Law Enforcement of exactly what you have been doing. I fancy that they will keep a very close eye on you for the foreseeable future."

If I could have curled up and disappeared, I would have done just that. He was quite right of course, we had been reckless, and foolish, and had nearly got ourselves killed.

I could see the Inspector back home, with whom we had previous dealings, making notes and nodding in agreement with the Super's assessment.

One thing was for sure, we'd have to keep a very low profile indeed for a long time.

It transpired, that when Robert had recovered from his latest collapse, he recalled that our exit from the hotel had seemed a little puzzling.

Thus, the Super informed us, he was pretty sure that we had been abducted.

By this time the interview room had filled up. There was a large number of tough-looking police, and two obviously senior officers.

It was rather exciting. I felt almost guilty that I was beginning to enjoy myself.

Somewhat abruptly, the Super told us to go back to the outer office.

Feeling a bit cowed we did as we were ordered. We found a couple of chairs, outside the custody suite, and sat there trying to appear nonchalant.

Finally, the Super emerged surrounded by the tough guys, at whom he was barking various orders.

When he'd finished, he walked over to us.

"Now then," he said, "against my better judgement, I'm going to ask you to accompany me back to the cottage you described. The lady in question may be perfectly innocent. It would be no surprise if she was, as I suspect that you Mrs. Standage have a vivid imagination."

I pinked up a little. It was quite true, but somehow I felt that it was not imagination in this case.

"However," he went on, "it is now, eight o'clock. We have arrangements to make, therefore we shall not be making our move until early tomorrow morning. So," one of his pauses, "it is probably advisable, that you get some sleep. I would suggest that you book yourselves into the local inn, and I shall send a WPC back to The Flowerdew to find you a change of clothing. Make a list of your requirements as quickly as possible

The inn proved to be a pleasant little pub/restaurant, which had a couple of rooms available for bed and breakfast. Neither of us were particularly hungry, but nevertheless we sat in the bar for half an hour or so, with a drink and a plateful of rather tasty sandwiches.

The WPC arrived with a suitcase containing the list of items I had left with the Super. We had to be ready by seven o'clock next morning, so we went to bed with all speed.

There was no time for breakfast. Just a cup of coffee.

Jack mumped and moaned, but frankly I couldn't have eaten anything, I was much too tense.

The Super breezed into the pub and barked, "I hope you're all prepared. I don't want to waste any time."

I made no comment, and allowed myself to be helped into the car. Jack winked at me, as the Super, still barking, climbed into the front passenger seat.

We drove quite swiftly, back in the direction of the cottage. As it came into view, the Super half turned in his seat.

"Under no circumstances are you to leave the car. I shall knock at the door and if the woman you suspect opens it, inform my officer. He'll take it from there."

I could feel a pout coming on, but I saw the sense in what he was saying. I was all agog as the Super approached the front door, and knocked.

After a few minutes the door opened a crack, and an elderly woman, bent almost double, looked out. The Super obviously asked her if there was anyone else in the house.

I could see her shaking her head in bewilderment.

After a further few minutes conversation, he turned away and came back to the car.

"Drive on, Jones," he said brusquely.

Jack and I looked at him.

"That poor old thing's being held hostage in her own home, or I miss my guess." He gazed straight ahead, without speaking again.

"Call for back up, and get someone to approach the house from the rear," he told Jones eventually.

"I fear," he said, "that your disappearance has been discovered by now, and there may be more innocent lives at stake, unless we move quickly."

Chapter Twenty-Nine

After that, it was all action. Constable Jones was an excellent driver, negotiating hairpin bends and blind corners with tremendous aplomb. I was very glad that Jack and I were strapped in on several occasions, as the car's tyres screamed on the road surface.

At last, the mansion came into view. My stomach did drop a little, but then I reminded myself that I was in the comparative safety of a police car.

There were already signs of a hefty police presence. A welter of cars, and other vehicles strategically parked. Quite a number of the officers seemed to be wearing protective vests, which made me swallow hard.

Was there going to be a shoot out, I wondered?

Watching police stakeouts in TV cop shows, it had often looked like overkill. But being there in the flesh, I would have been happy to see twice as many uniforms.

The Super had been barking orders, again, into his radio this time. He turned round and said severely, "Keep low if there's any action, and whatever you do, stay put!"

He and Jones jumped from the car, slamming the doors firmly closed. Jones set off at a run, followed at a very respectable pace by the Super.

There remained just a handful of men stationed outside. Jack and I clasped hands and sat gazing out of the windows, so as not to miss anything. After a few minutes a heavy set man emerged, hands cuffed behind his back.

There was a fair bit of shouting going on inside the house, but he was promptly thrust into one of the vans. We could hear him protesting that he was there to service the boiler and his employer would be furious at the way he was being treated. He was of course, ignored.

There were now just two uniformed men on guard. Jack and I waited.

Then, another flurry of activity as two rather nasty looking thugs were hustled out, hands behind, they too protesting their innocence. They were thrust into another van.

We waited again.

Now there was a lull. I pictured a line of large policemen climbing down the stairs under the floor, then picking their way along the passage.

Some of them would find it a bit cramped. I gave a nervous giggle. Jack looked at me.

"I was imagining some of those cops squeezing along the underground passage. If one got stuck, just think of the pile-up behind him?"

Jack smiled. "Pippsy, the Super said you had a vivid imagination – and you certainly have. Still, it would do well in one of the more light-hearted cop shows."

We settled down again. After a time I could feel my eyes growing heavy. The two uniforms left on guard duty were strolling around chatting. I would have loved to get out of the car and stretch my legs.

I looked over at Jack, he had leaned back and closed his eyes. So presently I joined him.

We must both have dozed off. I jerked awake at the sound of the car door opening, alas, it was not the law. Climbing into the front passenger seat was Dave, and to make matters worse he was flourishing a nasty looking gun. It was quite small, but had a dull finish which looked very menacing.

Jack had opened his eyes and looked less than happy.

Dave smiled slightly, "Now Mr. Standage, please join me in the front of the car. The driving seat to be exact. We're all going for a little ride, and in case you get any funny ideas, I shall be covering your lady wife at all times."

My heart knocked against my chest, and my stomach was in turmoil. This man had managed to avoid capture, and was obviously not going to hang around on the off chance. But what had happened to the two guards? There was no sign of them at all.

Jack climbed out very carefully, and even more carefully inserted himself into the driving seat.

Dave looked at him, "Very good Mr. Standage. Please start the engine and drive away from the house to the gates."

At the gates Jack was told to turn right.

"We shall be coming upon a cottage in due course. When we do, I shall expect you to pull up outside, switch off the engine, and give me the keys. Are we clear about that?" Dave was as unlike the man I knew as one of the 'fizzy foursome', as could possibly be imagined.

Having dropped his former persona, he revealed himself as dangerous, extremely so, I thought.

We drove back along the road we had so recently travelled. If we get out of this, I thought, I shall never criticise the Super again, even if we are only in this mess because he brought us along for the ride.

The chimney of the cottage appeared around the next bend. It was the cottage at which we had called yesterday.

I wondered what was next on the agenda. I didn't have to wait long. Dave took the keys, opened the rear door and indicated that I should get out.

Despite shaking legs, I managed to climb out with some dignity.

"You had better stay put Mr. Standage, unless you want something unpleasant to happen to your charming wife," he said.

He placed the gun gently against my back and urged me up the path to the front door. It swung open before we arrived. There stood the young woman, this time without the baby.

"What's she doing here?" she said.

"Insurance," Dave said drily.

"Her and a fella called here yesterday. Car had broken down or something. Mind you I was a bit suspicious, 'cos they took off all of a sudden. She said she'd left the car unlocked."

"Don't worry petal," he said. "She's staying here for a while, while I dump the car and until Mags arrives. She's very friendly with Mags. Mags'll get things sorted, and you can be on your way."

I didn't care for the sound of that. It struck me that Mags might be a ruthless woman, especially if her standard of living was being threatened.

The woman unlocked a door at the back of the house. It led into a large stone-flagged kitchen. I was not the only prisoner. There were two women sitting at the dining table. One, a young woman holding the baby, and the other the elderly woman I had seen earlier.

I heard the click as the door was re-locked.

The younger woman looked very frightened. "Who are you?" she asked.

"I'm Pippsy, my husband and I were brought here against our will by the man whose voice you can hear. We've got no idea what's going on, but I think that the police will be looking for us quite soon, especially as we drove here in a police car, so don't worry." I tried to sound calm and convincing, but I couldn't quite convince myself.

The elderly woman looked as though she was not quite with us. However, I couldn't have been more wrong.

"I'm Eva, and this is my granddaughter Joyce. The young man is my great grandson James, although we call him Jumbo, because he eats as much as an elephant. Didn't I see you in the car when that nice policeman called here a while back?"

I was taken aback. "Why, yes, yes you did," I stuttered.

"I tried to give the young man a hint that all was not as it should be. I had to be careful, because the woman, Marilyn she calls herself, was holding Joyce and Jumbo at knife point. I pretended I was not quite of this world, I'm afraid. I used to be an actress, many years ago."

"Well," I said, "you did very well indeed. The Superintendant who spoke to you, was very concerned. He was sure that you were being held against your will. I would say your performance was just about right."

We heard a voice call, "Mags'll be along soon." Then the slamming of the front door. My heart plummeted at the thought of my darling Jack being forced to go who knew where.

A couple of minutes later there was a hammering on the door, and Dave shouting something about, "The bloody man's disappeared!" Then the door slammed again.

The kitchen door opened and Marilyn looked at me, smirking.

"Your fella's done a runner. Sir Galahad he surely ain't!"

With that she shut and locked the door again.

I looked at Eva and Joyce. "Whatever she said my husband won't have "done a runner". He'll have a plan so we'd better prepare ourselves."

Joyce looked bewildered, but Eva was smiling. I had the feeling that she was almost enjoying herself.

I paced around the kitchen. It was very well equipped. A magnificent Aga, above which was an array of gleaming copper saucepans, and a Welsh dresser displaying dishes, plates, cups and saucers.

In one corner was a door which led into a walk-in pantry come utility room, and in the opposite corner was the door leading out into the garden. This of course was also locked.

"That was the first door they locked," Eva said. "Although, where they thought we could go I don't know. An old biddy and a woman with a baby? Could you see us scampering across the fields in our slippers? I don't think so."

I was beginning to like Eva more and more. One day, when this was all over, I was going to sit down and listen to her life story. At least, I told myself, I'm thinking positively about this being all over.

I continued pacing, stopping every so often to look out of the window. As might be expected the garden was filled with beds of flowering shrubs, and a little flagged path wound its way hither and yon. At the end of the garden was a small orchard, and to one side a large greenhouse. At any other time I would have loved to wander round that garden. As it was, I was busy trying to work out some way of getting out there in the first place.

I examined the window. However, being a cottage window, it was a bit on the small side. Too small for me to contemplate climbing through. Eva would have had difficulty, despite her small size, and I somehow couldn't quite picture her wriggling through, then going in search of something hefty to smash the door down.

No, I must just hope that Jack had come up with a plan, which he was putting into action at that very moment.

As if on cue, he appeared at the window. My heart leapt. We would be safe now, Jack was here. Then he disappeared.

I was so disappointed I could have wept.

He appeared at the door, a few seconds later. The door was very thick and heavy, but had a small glass panel at the top, which Jack seemed to be scratching.

Eva was already there trying to mouth something, without being too loud.

"Let me," I said, "Jack and I have our own code."

Eva watched carefully as Jack and I communicated, using a combination of hand signals and lip reading techniques.

"Where did you learn all that," she asked, when Jack finally moved away.

"From a client, who was deaf. We're no experts, but it's proved useful now and again, I can tell you."

I was thinking of the message Jack had given me, and what I could do to help.

"Listen carefully you two," I said. "I knew Jack would have a plan, and he has. You Eva, are going to have to draw on all your acting skills. Pretend to have a fit, or a heart attack or something, whatever you can manage. And Joyce, you've got to scream blue murder, while I'll be getting ready to jump on the Marilyn woman, as soon as she gets into the room."

"How, how can you be sure she'll even open the door?" Joyce quavered.

"Because, you're going to scream words like, 'Help, murder, dial 999, she's dying'. Be as dramatic as you like."

"Oh dear, I don't know if I can do it." Joyce was beginning to get on my nerves. I was about to tell her to sort herself out when Eva snapped, "Pull yourself together. Don't be such a washout. If I'm going to act my socks off, so must you. Now get on with it, as soon as Pippsy gives us the nod."

"Jack's going to go to the front door, and hammer on it while we're carrying on and creating in here. With any luck that woman'll drop her guard, and we should be able to take her."

Eva rubbed her hands. "Yes, I would like to give her what for."

We arranged ourselves. Eva flat on the floor opposite the door, Joyce on her knees beside her, after popping Jumbo into his highchair. I positioned myself so that I would be behind the door as it opened.

"Jack is going to tap on the kitchen window then we count to twenty and launch into our performance."

It seemed an age. Joyce moaned that her knees were killing her. Jumbo sat in his highchair, sucking on a rusk and grinning all over his face. We must have looked a comical lot.

At last came the tap I'd been waiting for. I began counting, slowly Jack had said, but not too slowly.

"Eighteen, nineteen, twenty, here we go." Joyce really let rip. I didn't think she had it in her, while Eva was moaning and groaning as if she were at her last gasp. I could hear Marilyn shouting, something about, 'stopping that racket or I'll do for you', then Jack began hammering on the door.

The kitchen door was unlocked and the woman came in at a run.

"Shut your silly face, you – what's the matter with her, is she dying or something?"

I slammed the door behind her, and leapt for her back. Eva sat up and head butted her in the stomach, while Joyce, who was rocketting up in my estimation, grabbed her ears and twisted them.

She dropped onto the floor yelling. I, of course, landed on top of her, which made her yell even louder.

"The front door!" I shouted. Joyce ran for her life, and yanked it open. My darling Jack burst in, and stopped in the doorway. A huge grin spread across his face.

"You don't need me then," he said. "She won't be going anywhere."

He was right. The wretched woman seemed to have passed out, she must have hit her head when she fell. I stood up breathing hard.

He gave his hand gallantly to Eva, who was struggling to stand.

She looked him up and down.

"So you're Pippsy's husband. It is nice to meet you, though I wish the circumstances could have been more hospitable."

Jack proceeded to take charge. "Where is your telephone, ma'am?"

"That's in the sitting room, follow me," Eva said graciously.

Joyce looked at me. "What shall we do with her?" she asked.

"Find something to tie her up, I think," I said, looking around. "Is there any washing line or strong string anywhere?"

Joyce stood biting her lip. "Grandma's got a drawer in the dresser, full of odds and ends, there could be something in there."

We opened the drawer, keeping an eye on the recumbant Marilyn. Joyce groped around amongst the jumble of thimbles, rolls of sellotape, spare greeting cards, old notelet pads and the like. Right at the back she unearthed a ball of stout twine. The kind of thing that gardeners use for plants. Just the job.

Marilyn's eyes were flickering as we got to work on her.

"We'd better not tie it too tightly," Joyce whispered, "or we'll cut off the blood supply."

"I suppose," I said glumly. As far as I was concerned, the woman's blood supply was the last thing to worry about.

By this time she was coming round, and finding her voice again. There was a fine flow of language when she realised her plight. Threats to the effect that we'd be mincemeat when her boyfriend caught up with us.

Joyce looked a little perturbed, but I told her that Marilyn's boyfriend was probably being rounded up by the police at that very moment. This seemed to settle her nerves.

She plucked Jumbo out of the highchair and headed for the sitting room.

"Oy, you can't leave me here like this," Marilyn screeched.

I turned and looked at her for a long moment. "That," I said smirking, much as she had done, "is exactly what we can do, and what's more we're doing it."

I slammed the door closed and turned the key. She was a slippery customer, I didn't doubt, and I was sure that she would already be trying to find a way out of her predicament.

In the sitting room, Jack was on the phone telling someone exactly where we were. Eva was sitting in a chair. She looked a bit pale. I wondered if her exertions had taken too much out of her. Gutsy or not, one had to remember that she was an elderly woman.

Joyce bent down beside her.

"Are you O.K. Grandma?"

Eva nodded. "Just a little winded that's all. I haven't been called upon to stage such an act for very many years. Get the brandy out of the cupboard, and we'll all have a snifter."

"Do you think you should, Grandma? If you're feeling a bit dicky you should lie down."

Eva dismissed that with a wave of her little hand. "Don't be wet Joyce. I really don't know why you're always so feeble. Doesn't come from my side of the family that's certain. Now do what I said, get the brandy, there's a good girl."

Three small glasses of brandy were poured, Joyce of course declining.

Eva sniffed. "Hmph, I can see you take after your father when it comes to pouring drinks. He's always as tight fisted as they come. Anyway it's my brandy, so let's have something worth swallowing."

Reluctantly, Joyce topped the glasses up, mumbling, "If Mum knew about this, she'd kill me. She says that you're too fond of a drink."

"Pah, what she doesn't know won't hurt. And I hardly think that a snifter of brandy of an evening constitutes the royal road to alcoholism."

I was listening to this exchange, and trying hard to keep a straight face.

Jack meanwhile had finished his phone call, and sipped gratefully.

"The officer I spoke to said the Super's phone seemed to be out of range, but he thinks it's only a matter of time before he turns up at the station. That being the case, for safety's sake we should perhaps, post a lookout. It's possible that we might have a visit from more of the gang if they've managed to evade capture. Or maybe even someone not at the house to begin with."

My stomach gave a little heave, as I remembered what Marilyn had said about her boyfriend.

"Your best bet," Eva said, "is to post yourself at the front or back bedroom windows. Or maybe both, to be on the safe side. No one can get near without being seen from the bedrooms."

We arranged that Jack would do the front bedroom, while I was at the rear. The threat which just a few minutes ago had receded, suddenly loomed large again.

Once in position, I felt more reassured. Eva was right there was a clear view all around the garden. Anyone sneaking through the trees would be spotted immediately.

Jack called, "I don't think anyone could approach without my seeing them. I can see right over the hedge, so a car pulling up wouldn't be hidden either."

We settled down. I wondered what Marilyn was up to. I felt sure that she wouldn't be content to just lie there waiting.

Time passed. Why didn't the police arrive? Surely the Super should have got the message by now.

I looked at my watch for the umpteenth time. It was nearly half an hour since Jack and I had come upstairs. I wondered if Eva had bucked up, and if Joyce had settled her conscience with regard to the brandy.

"Jack!" I called. "What do you think's happening back at the mansion?"

"Who knows?" was the reply. He didn't elaborate – always a bad sign with Jack. He's worried, I thought.

More time passed. I looked at my watch again, another fifteen minutes at least had gone by. If only we had some idea what was happening.

I felt as though my eyes were drying up. Then I saw them.

One minute the garden was empty, the next, the Fizzy Foursome were moving purposefully around, by the greenhouse.

"Jack, quick, come in here," I called. He came at a run.

"Look," I pointed.

"Blimey, where did they come from? We've got to do something. Sharpish!"

"Yes, but what?" I squeaked. Why does my voice always squeak when I'm agitated?

"Run down, and get the others up here, I've got an idea," Jack said.

I was down those stairs like lightening.

"Come on troops, upstairs, soonest. We've got company."

Joyce moaned and clasped baby Jumbo tightly. Eva struggled out of the chair and made her way upstairs, with admirable speed. Joyce trailed behind saying, "Oh dear, Oh dear," over and over again.

On the landing Jack had opened the loft cover and pulled down the ladder. I hadn't realised that there was a loft.

"We've got to get up there, and stay quiet, because if they suspect we're still here, I think that'll be it."

I swallowed, hard. With a bit of pushing and shoving and the help of the rickety ladder, we got Eva, and Joyce and the baby into the loft. Jack gave me a bunk up, then swung himself up with ease. He pulled the ladder up and closed the cover. I thought, thank heavens for low, cottage ceilings.

It was a typical under eaves space. High enough in the centre to stand upright, and sloping away sharply on each side.

"Lie flat. As far away from the cover as possible," Jack said.

There was a box at the gable end, and Jack made his way over to it.

The gods must have been smiling, as it was full of old blankets and bedding. We unloaded it, then lay down covering ourselves as much as possible, piling the blankets on and around our bodies.

"With any luck, this lot will muffle any creaks, and if they do decide to investigate, we must cover our faces, and hope for the best." Jack had it all worked out.

We lay as still as possible. Luckily Jumbo dropped off to sleep while Joyce cuddled him. It was nerve wracking, however, just lying there listening.

We heard the sound of voices, a babble in fact. They'd discovered Marilyn.

I could hear her screeching away, and the language was terrible. I thought I'd heard it all, but there was some that made even me blush.

Presently there was the sound of footsteps on the stairs. This was it. I found I was praying that Jumbo wouldn't wake up, or that the dust wouldn't cause one of us to sneeze.

I recognised Mags's voice.

"Nothing up here," she shouted. "I reckon they've legged it down the lane towards the village. They can't have got far."

There was another jumble of conversation, then Dave shouted, "We've got to get going, the filth'll be on us if we're not careful. We'll catch up with the buggers if we drive fast."

There was another babble of sound, then the slamming of the door. All fell silent.

Joyce sat up and breathed a huge sigh, "Thank goodness, we can go now....." but Jack put his finger to his lips.

"It could be a con. They could've either left someone behind, or be sitting downstairs, just waiting for us to appear."

It was all too feasible. Joyce groaned and lay down again.

We lay there for a long time. So long in fact, that I fell asleep again. I was jerked awake by Jack shaking my shoulder.

"I'm going to open the cover and have a shufti. If there is anyone down there, they might be thinking that we have got away, after all this time."

I clutched his hand. "Be careful, don't take any chances, and take something with you that could be a useful weapon."

"Like what?" Jack asked, reasonably enough I suppose.

"There's got to be something you could make use of," I said, looking around the loft. It was difficult to see up here, although it wasn't pitch black. There must have been a couple of loose tiles, as there was a definite glimmer of light from somewhere.

Jack had a careful creep around, then said, "Ah hah! Success!"

He turned, holding what looked like a piece of wood, but turned out to be a baseball bat.

"Where did that come from," I whispered.

"There's a box here, I didn't see it before, but it seems to have various items of sports gear in it. There are a couple of golf clubs, but I reckon this bat will do nicely."

Eva and Joyce were stirring and groaning a bit. So they must have slept too.

"What's the plan?" Eva asked.

Jack told them.

"Are you sure it's safe?" Joyce said in a trembling tone.

"No," Jack said, "but it's no good staying here any longer. If they've all gone we can leave and try to find the cops. The chances are, if they haven't found us on the road, they're going to come back, and mount a more thorough search. Now I don't know about you, but I don't fancy that too much, do you?"

Eva looked grave. "No, young man, I don't fancy that, as you put it."

He went over to the cover, and slowly and cautiously moved it aside. He lowered himself onto the landing.

"If it's all clear, I'll be back, so get ready."

My heart was in my mouth as he eased himself down the stairs. I was lying flat by this time with my head hanging out of the loft opening. I could hear myself whispering, "Be careful, be careful," terrified of what I might hear.

It was very quiet. Oh lord, I thought, he's been stabbed or knocked unconscious, there'll be someone creeping up the stairs to do for us any minute. Yes, someone was creeping up the stairs, it was Jack.

"Come on troops," he said, "I reckon we haven't got long, before they'll be back."

We scrambled out of the loft somehow with the ladder shaking and rattling. The baby had woken up by this time, and was fractious.

"He needs to be fed," Joyce said firmly. "I shall fetch his bottle, and he can have it as we go along."

So, Jumbo was popped into his buggy, securely strapped in and handed his bottle. His little face lit up. He was very adept at feeding himself.

When I queried this with Joyce she said, "He's eleven months, and he wants to do things for himself, it's a bit messy at times, but he loves it."

We left with great care.

"Now," Jack said, "which would be the most inconspicuous route to take to the village?"

"Across the fields behind the house," Eva said. "It will take us to the church, and I know the vicar very well, so we can hide out there while he calls the police."

There was a little footpath by the side of the house, which led directly to the fields. We had a bit of a shermozzle getting the buggy plus baby, over the stile, but a good concerted effort did the trick.

Luckily the fields were lying fallow. No crops, no cattle, and very little mud, it made for safer easier walking.

Another plus was that the day was overcast, which could have made it more difficult for anyone to spot us, should they have been looking.

After starting out at a brisk enough pace Eva began to flag.

"I'm not as agile as I once was," she explained. "A touch of arthritis in my knees I'm afraid. It does slow me down."

With great gallantry Jack held out his arm, and proceeded to guide her over the ground with care.

The journey was not as far as I feared. The spire of the church poked up above a clump of trees after about fifteen minutes.

"We will come to the churchyard, and the rectory is just beyond," Eva said.

Five minutes later we were picking our way through gravestones, some of which dated back a couple of hundred years, Eva told us. The rectory which was a rather ugly building, had a couple of lights shining.

It was squat and square, resembling a child's drawing of a house, but for me, at that moment it was the most beautiful house I had ever seen.

Eva climbed onto the front step and pressed the bell. I could hear Westminster chimes. A second or two later a plump, rather untidy woman, who turned out to be the rector's wife, opened the door to us.

"Eva, my dear, you looked fagged out. Come in, come in. Joyce, is that you? And Jumbo too, how lovely. Are these relatives or friends? Go into the sitting room, I'll put the kettle on you'll want tea of course. Sit down my dears, make yourselves at home, I shan't be long. David's over at the church, but he'll be back any time now."

Under other circumstances I might have described the woman as gushing. But not today. Today she epitomised warmth and hospitality. I could have thrown myself on her bosom and wept.

Eva put her hand on the woman's arm. "Miranda, we'd love some tea, but we'd also love to make use of your phone if we may. It's a long story, but we can tell you over that cup of tea."

Jack was shown back into the hall, and pointed in the direction of the phone. Talking all the while, Miranda disappeared into the kitchen at the back of the house.

Eva looked at me, "I'm afraid she does go on a bit, but she's one of the kindest people I think I've ever met."

I nodded. At that moment, Miranda was a saint for my money.

Chapter Thirty

David, the vicar arrived about ten minutes later. By this time, Eva and I were informing Miranda of our adventures to date.

He was a short, pleasant faced man who listened to our tale with appropriate expressions of shock, surprise, distress and horror.

"You youngsters, and our dear friends Eva and Joyce, have had a most traumatic time," he said. "It's incredible that such things should be happening just a few minutes from our front door."

We were all agreed on that.

Jack had somehow managed to get a word with the Super, who assured him that he would be with us very soon. I wondered what 'very soon' meant. My main worry, and I think Jack's too, was that the Foursome would soon realise that we had found refuge somewhere. It wouldn't take them too long to work out, that the Rectory was the nearest house to the cottage.

Neither of us vouchsafed this choice piece of information to the others. But David proved much more astute than his appearance suggested.

"It could be," he said, "that the people whom you describe as the Foursome, will come looking for you here. I think therefore, the best place for all of you is the crypt. Don't be concerned," he held up a hand, "modern crypts are quite different these days. Ours is often the venue for concerts, so it's well equipped with heating, lighting, comfortable seating and facilities for making beverages."

Miranda was nodding her head. "I'll give you some blankets. The heating won't take long to warm up, but it might be a little fresh to start with."

Her expression was so comforting that once again, I could have thrown myself into her arms.

We were soon ensconced in the church crypt, which was surprisingly bright and welcoming.

"It will be necessary to lock you in, just for safety's sake," David told us. "If we do have unwelcome visitors, this is the last place we want them to look. I can stall them I'm sure by acting innocent. I'm quite good at that." He grinned, and Miranda chuckled.

After our hosts had gone, we made ourselves comfortable on the upholstered pews. It was obvious that no expense had been spared on upgrading what must once have been a dismal place.

I wondered, out loud, where the funds had come from.

Eva told us that a wealthy parishioner had donated £50,000. It seemed that when his mother was dying, both David and Miranda had visited her every day to support and comfort her. Out of gratitude, when the old lady was gathered to her reward, her son suggested there should be a lasting memorial to her. The modern crypt was the outcome.

"It's called St. Mary's crypt," Eva said. "The woman's name was Mary, but by all accounts she was a bad tempered, miserable old bat, so the saint bit was stretching it. I reckon her son's gratitude was down to the fact that he'd seen the last of her."

Despite our predicament, we all laughed at Eva's caustic summing up.

We sat talking on and off for a while, until we heard the sound of the door being unlocked. David came in smiling.

"As we suspected, your friends finally found their way to our door. The man who seemed to be in charge was a rather unsavoury character, I thought. Tried to bully his way into the house, insisting that they were police looking for criminals posing as a family. I thought he was going to force his way in at one point, but one of the woman said something to him, and he backed off. My gut feeling is, that they won't have gone far, so until the real police arrive, you'd better stay put."

"We shouldn't put you in danger," Jack said. "In fact, I think Pippsy and I should make a run for it. If the Foursome come back and won't take no for an answer, you all stand a better chance, if we're not here."

My heart sank at Jack's words, but I knew he was right. The people Dave wanted most were us. We knew too much, and therefore were the most dangerous. I feared a little for Eva and Joyce, but something told me that they were just a side issue, as far as Dave was concerned.

David started to argue, but Jack would have none of it.

"You've already done too much," he said. "Take care of the others, and we'll get going to try and find the Super. He must surely be on his way."

I hugged Eva and Joyce, and kissed the top of Jumbo's head. We thanked David, and Miranda who had appeared by this time, then taking a very careful look outside first, we left.

It was beginning to get dark now, as we picked our way carefully through the graveyard.

"I think," Jack said, "that we should try for the police station. If we keep close to the hedges we can always drop down, if a car comes along."

"Whatever," I said shakily. "If, I mean, when we get out of this, I'm going to find myself a really safe job. A mining engineer, or a deep sea diver or something." My voice cracked with a sob.

Jack gave me a cuddle. "Come on Pipps, chin up, this is the worst scrape we've been in I know, but we'll come through, you'll see."

I snivelled a bit, blew my nose, and took a pull at myself. "Sorry sweetheart," I said, "I'll tough it out somehow."

"That's my girl."

We'd reached the main road, so with several deep breaths and hugging the verge, we started for the village.

Eventually the police station appeared. Oh thank the lord, I thought, we'll be O.K. now.

Vain hope. There were no lights burning, and the doors were locked. We stood there hammering on them for a few moments.

"It's no use," Jack said at last. "They're all home, enjoying their supper, and CSI or Midsomer Murders on TV."

"What do we do now?" I said.

Jack was pulling his lip. "We'll try one of the other houses, and find out where the village bobbies live."

He'd barely got the words out, when we heard the sound of a car coming from the direction we had just walked.

Like mad things we ran to the back of the building, and dived into the undergrowth. The car kept going, so perhaps it wasn't our nasty friends. All the same, I was unhappy at the thought of leaving our cover. Still we couldn't stay here in hopes. The station was probably closed for the night, and who knew what might come roaming around in the dark.

We crept back to the road. There was no sign of a car, so we began walking towards the cluster of houses that made up the village's main street.

We stopped at the first one and looked it over. A small well kept garden, fresh paintwork, and best of all, lights!

There was a doorknocker in the shape of a key, and a bellpush set into the doorframe. Deep breath time again. Jack pressed the bell.

A few seconds later the door opened, the woman standing there had the light behind her, but I recognised that voice, "Oh, we've been expecting you, do come in."

It was Mags.

Chapter Thirty-One

I could have dropped on the spot. After all we'd been through, we'd delivered ourselves right into their hands.

Jools appeared in the doorway, and she and Mags grabbed our arms and hustled us inside.

Both husbands were seated in the sitting room into which we were thrust.

"Well, Mr. and Mrs. Standage, at last. You've led us a merry dance, I must say." Dave was sitting in an armchair by the open fire, nursing a glass of what looked like scotch.

"How did we manage to miss you? I'm really interested to hear. You've been quite smart. Up until now that is."

"When we left the cottage, we just took off, and dodged around," Jack told him.

"You didn't by any chance call on the vicar did you?"

"What vicar?" I chipped in. "We haven't even seen a church, let alone a vicar. We've been too busy dodging."

I hoped he'd believe me. I was giving it my all!

He looked at me steadily then shrugged. "Well, it doesn't matter now. I'd hoped, when we were in conversation the other day that you might be interested in throwing in your lot with me. I quite took to you both. Enterprising, if a little foolhardy perhaps, but you could have been very useful, especially as you have a penchant for making friends with policemen."

I couldn't believe my ears. Could he really have believed that we'd have joined him in his nefarious doings?

"As I said, it doesn't matter now. Your precious Superintendant's a bit late in finding you, but when he does, well, you won't be telling him anything, and we'll be long gone."

He nodded to Mags and Jools.

The two women advanced upon us with a determined air.

"You won't try something stupid, will you? Mags and Jools are quite useful with the martial arts, aren't you girls?"

They smirked. We were marched out, and into an adjoining room. There wasn't much furniture, just a couple of upright chairs.

"See you later," Mags chortled, as they left.

The ominous sound of the door being locked followed.

Jack and I looked at each other in despair.

"This, I think, is probably going to be it," Jack said at last.

I nodded. I couldn't bring myself to speak.

We looked around the room. There was an inglenook fireplace that looked as though it had been manufactured six months ago. The window was shuttered, and the door had more bolts, bars and locks than the Jewel House at the Tower.

All in all, not too promising. Still, I was determined not to break down again. My natural optimism began to rise.

"If they're planning to get rid of us, they're not going to do it here. We've got to think of some way of fighting back when they come to get us."

Jack pulled his lip again. "If the ladies are martial arts experts, we might have a problem."

I nodded. Neither Jack nor I were much for aggressive sports. But my blood was beginning to boil. This was the third time we'd been locked up at the pleasure of these monsters, and I was getting sick of it.

The chairs were an interesting design. Hefty wood frames and thick solid seats. They wouldn't have looked out of place in a mediaeval castle.

"There's got to be some way of dismantling these things," I said pointing.

Jack looked a bit bemused. "Without a hammer, or at the very least a heavy screwdriver, I can't see us having much success."

I looked around the room again, seeking something that would serve as tool.

In the fireplace was a set of fire irons. I picked up the sturdy poker. It had a sharp point, so perhaps we could somehow lever one or two legs off.

I suggested it to Jack. He picked up the poker and had a go at pushing it between the leg and seat of the chair. After straining and heaving for several minutes, he wiped his forehead and sat down.

"That's a no go then," I said.

"Perhaps we could use the poker itself as a weapon," I mused.

"As what? A jousting lance?"

"The shovel's heavy enough to use as a club," I said, ignoring him.

He threw up his hands. "By the time we get our act together, they'll be on us and we'll be dragged out kicking and screaming."

"We've got to do something," I almost stamped my foot. "I for one don't intend to be dragged anywhere, kicking, screaming or otherwise. Now come on love, if we think hard enough, we must come up with something."

"Well," Jack said eventually, "it looks like the fire irons or nothing. We might as well give it a go, we've got nothing to lose."

I grabbed the shovel, as Jack took the poker. We stationed ourselves on either side of the door. My gut feeling told me, we probably wouldn't have to wait long.

Sure enough a few minutes later we heard the tap, tap of high heels along the floor outside.

"This is it," I whispered.

The key turned and the door was pushed slowly open. Whoever it was, was taking no chances.

It was Mags.

I leapt at her waving the shovel, but she seemed unfazed. She put her finger to her lips, and pulled the door closed.

"Don't make a sound," she said. "We've got to get out of here as quickly as we can."

I must have looked as amazed as I felt.

"It's O.K.," she said. "I've got a plan. My car's parked round the back, and I've got a key for the back door. They don't know that I've got that key or that I'm even in here. I said I was going to shower. They're having a couple of drinks. Celebrating I shouldn't wonder, if they're planning on getting rid of you."

While she talked, she was undoing the back door. We followed her out into the pitch dark garden. Luckily there was no sign of any security lights, so we were able to make a dash for it.

At the back of the house there was hard standing. Two cars were parked there, one of which was the BMW. Mags unlocked it.

"Get in quick," she hissed. "A shower doesn't take that long. If I know Dave, he'll be up to see what's happened to me."

We scrambled into the back, as Mags started the engine. She reversed and turned the car with a speed which would have had a Grand Prix driver gawping in admiration.

We hammered off through the village.

"Where are we going?" I asked.

"To find your friendly copper," she said shortly.

"D'you know where to look?" Jack said.

"You bet," was the reply.

After that, we sat in silence, as Mags drove as if we were competitors in the Monte Carlo Rally.

I'd always considered myself a reasonably good driver, but Mags left me standing. Hedges appeared to flash by, and she cornered and twisted with an air of cool competence.

At last we were on the outskirts of Cheltenham. I expected Mags to ease off a bit, but that didn't seem to be in her grand scheme of things. We finally screeched to a halt, outside a building which bore the most welcome sign I could ever hope to see – Police!

Mags was out and up the steps, and we followed at a run. Before we had time to draw breath, she was demanding to speak to Superintendant Fitzgerald.

The young PC behind the desk looked petrified. "Yes, Ma'am, of course, at once," he babbled.

He rapidly punched in a number on the switchboard.

"Sir, sir, a lady must see you immediately, and there's another couple with her who could be the people we've been looking for. I think you should come, sir. Really I do."

Whatever the response, it satisfied him as he smiled at us, albeit rather shakily and said, "The Superintendant will be with you at once, if you'd just like to take a seat."

He was as good as his word. A door behind the desk opened, and my hero Super Cop emerged.

"Rustle up some tea, lad," he said. "Now if you'll just follow me ladies and gentleman, we'll go somewhere for a nice little chat."

When we were all seated, in a quite comfortable interview room, with mugs of tea in our hands, he did his steepling of the fingers and said, "Right now, fire away, as soon as you like."

Before Jack or I could say a word, Mags began speaking.

We listened almost open mouthed.

"Dave and me, we've been married for fifteen years. I knew he was a bit dodgy when I met him, but he was a looker and I fancied him, so as it was only ducking and diving I thought it was a bit of a laugh really.

"I mean, we've made a packet now and again, been able to live the dream, as they say, but he's changed over the last year or two. Met people from abroad and got big ideas. Sees himself as a major player or something. I went along with it for a bit, but I draw the line at some things, and murder's one of them.

"It all started with those bleeding diamonds. Some bloke from Spain or France or somewhere gave them to him to get rid of. I knew it wasn't right. I told him so, but would he listen? No. So some other bloke pinches them and Dave's in a sweat, 'cos they're not his. Then there's all this business with the counterfeiting. I thought we were buying the hotel to start a new life. Some hopes. 'The hotel's a front' he says. 'There's much more at stake,' he says. 'If everything goes according to plan, we'll be multi billionaires, and the world'll be our playground,' he says.

"I don't want any of that, I told him, I just want a quiet life. Running an hotel would suit me very well. He wouldn't have it, wasn't interested. He's not the man I married. We had so much fun, but now he's only interested in money. Even when we first came here, we were still having a good time, us and Jools and Bill. I didn't know the half of it. I must have really been in la la land."

She stopped talking suddenly, and put her face in her hands. I could hear faint sobs.

The Super had nodded his way through all she had said.

I felt sorry for her. She didn't have a lovely guy like my Jack, and the shock must have been tremendous when she discovered what Dave was really like. After fifteen years too!

The Super stood up.

"We must deal with this at once. You will all have to remain here, it is not safe for you to be wandering about."

"But, what happened at the mansion?" I asked eagerly.

"I don't have time to talk about that. My first priority is to round up the three people who have been causing you," he looked at Jack and me, "so much bother."

As he strode out of the room we could hear him in barking mode once again.

The three of us sat looking firstly at the floor, then at each other.

"I'm really sorry you've had so much trouble," Mags said. "If I'd have known what was going on, I'd have tipped you the wink, then you could have moved on, but I thought you were there for a holiday, like us."

I thought we were too, I felt like saying.

The young PC came bustling in.

"The Superintendant told me to look after you. Would you care for some food? The canteen's closed, but I could send out for something."

Mags shook her head, and the thought of food turned my stomach. Jack however, brightened up considerably.

"I could fancy a take away. A curry perhaps?" he ended hopefully.

"I'm sure we could arrange that. What can I get for the ladies?"

Mags shook her head again, and mopped her eyes. I felt a little sorry for the young man so I said, "I'll have a sandwich, if it's not too much trouble."

He beamed, "What sort of filling?"

"Anything at all really," I said. "I'm not that hungry."

He left the room at a gallop.

Jack had the nerve to rub his hands. "A bit of curry would go down a treat. Plus a pint. You don't think they could run to that as well do you?"

I was dumbstruck, but not for long. "Jack Standage, you are the end. This poor woman is suffering here, and you're talking about pints."

"It's only one p....."

"Shut up!" I told him.

Mags looked at us mournfully. "Dave and I used to be just like you. When we were first married we had so many laughs." She stopped, sighing.

I didn't know what to say.

"Perhaps he was led astray somehow," I attempted.

"Led astray? No, I think it must always have been in him, just waiting for the right moment. I did love him though."

She stopped and sighed again.

The door opened, and the young PC came in carrying a tray.

"I got you chicken salad," he put a plate of reasonable looking sandwiches down in front of me.

"And the Tandoori do a nice chicken korma, hope that'll suit?" he passed over the tray holding a container of curry and one of rice.

I must admit the curry smelled and looked good. Even Mags was looking slightly envious.

"Can I get you anything else?"

"Weeel...." Jack began, but I leapt in, "Three cups of your delicious tea, would be perfect."

Chapter Thirty-Two

We all felt better after a little food. Mags had been persuaded to have a spoonful of curry and a sandwich.

There was a flurry of activity going on outside the interview room. I ventured to peep out once or twice, but it was useless. Plainclothes and uniformed officers were hurrying up and down the corridor, some flourishing sheafs of papers, others talking into their phones.

Occasionally I heard what I assumed were orders being shouted. They must have been orders, because anyone in the corridor immediately broke into a sprint.

Now that we were calmer, I began to wish I was part of it. It looked quite exciting, and bearing in mind how involved we'd become, I wanted to be in at the kill.

For two pins I would have strolled out casually, and had a try at getting some information. But when I suggested this to Jack he almost had a fit, and Mags looked horrified.

"Any sign of us trying to muscle in on the action, and we'll be spending the night in one of the unoccupied cells," Jack said.

I supposed he was right, but it was a pity. We'd come this far, and been in so many scrapes surely it was only right that we should at least, know what was happening.

The three of us sat attempting to make conversation. Mags told us a little more about the slightly nefarious activities that had occupied Dave and herself a few years ago.

As she'd said, they'd been very small beer for the most part. Their speciality was a scam involving personalised number plates. Apparently they would advertise in the more upmarket magazines, and the internet, purporting to have several rare, much sought after plates. She said the punters had fallen over themselves to bid higher and higher, to acquire one of these fictitious plates.

She and Dave would accept the highest bid then disappear. As they were using false names and addresses each time, they managed to pull it off easily.

Of course, all good things come to an end, and eventually the police got on their trail.

"We popped over to the Continent for a year or two," she told us. "Just until things cooled down, and anyway there were some rich pickings over there. We did all right," she finished wistfully, "the people we scammed could well afford it, and it gave us a very nice lifestyle."

They'd returned home after a while, as Mags's father was ill, and her mother needed support.

"We actually went straight after Dad died," she said. "Dave knew a bit about cars, and he'd met Bill by this time, so they opened up a dealership. Did O.K. too. It wasn't enough for Dave though, he met these blokes that talked him into all kinds of schemes. Then Jools decided she wanted a slice. For all she seems to be an airhead, she's real smart and she dragged Bill into it. That cottage we were in is one of a string, all over the country. She rents them out on a short lease, then uses them when there's business in that area. I didn't know the half of it, not until a few days ago. She wanted that old lady's cottage, and was trying to bully her into selling. Poor soul. I was disgusted with the way she was treated, which was another reason for me to want out."

I felt even more sorry for her.

"What will you do now?" I asked.

"Provided they get banged up, I might run the dealership. I've been a bit dumb about the other stuff, but I've got a good head for business, and I reckon I could do alright."

The door opened and a young WPC popped her head in.

"All O.K.?" she said.

"Well, actually, no," I said before Jack or Mags could speak. "What's happening? We've been here for ages, and no one's said anything about anything."

She looked at us nonplussed. "I'm afraid I can't help you. The Super's out and about, but he'll be back later. Perhaps he'll talk to you then. Now can I get you anything? Tea? Coffee?"

Jack brightened up.

"A pint wouldn't go amiss," he told her, flashing his smile.

She flushed and shuffled her feet. "I don't think I could get you a pint, sir. Sorry. I'll bring you some coffee shall I?"

With that she opened the door and left looking purposeful.

I'd had enough. I jumped up and said, "Must go to the loo or I'll burst."

I darted out before Mags could say she wanted to go too.

The loo however was the last place I intended to visit. Trying to make as little sound as possible I ran down the corridor towards the main entrance area.

Apart from the officer behind the desk, it was deserted. Now what? He looked up at that moment and caught sight of me lurking.

"Can I help at all?"

"Er, I was looking for the ladies powder room." Why on earth I phrased it like that I couldn't imagine.

The officer grinned. "The 'powder room' is down that way." He pointed to another corridor off to the right.

I thanked him with a big smile, and took off as if the matter was urgent.

I was faced with half a dozen doors. Ladies and Gents, of course. Then, the Super's office. I knew it was his, because it said so on the door.

That left three unmarked doors.

I put my ear to one. Couldn't hear a thing.

Very cautiously I opened it. This was the door to the stairs, both up and down. Taking a breath, I started climbing. As I reached the next floor, I heard voices.

Oh gawd, I thought. What on earth am I going to say?

However, the voices faded. I tried to swallow, but my mouth was dry.

I pushed open the connecting door and found a similar corridor to that on the floor below. Which way, which way?

There was a group of four doors up here, so I trotted off in the opposite direction.

I don't know what I expected to find, or what I was going to do if I found it. But what happened was a shock and then some. At the end of the corridor was a pair of glass doors, they swung open and a man marched through. It was Crichton!

"You!" it was involuntary. My first instinct was to take to my heels, except, there wouldn't be anywhere to run.

"Well, if it isn't Mrs. Standage. What a delightful surprise." He gave me a superior smile.

This is the end, I thought. I don't know how he managed to find us, but he's obviously here to finish us off. Oh Jack, what have I done?

He strolled up to me, holding out his hand. I couldn't believe it, he actually expected me to shake hands with him.

"You look scared to death," he said. Very unfortunate turn of phrase, I thought.

"Don't worry, things are not always as they seem," he went on. "But, I suspect that you should not be prowling around up here. You're too impetuous. Does your husband know where you are? No," he answered himself, "of course he doesn't."

"I think," he said, "that I had better take you back to where you came from. Then, we must have a serious talk."

It sounded ominous, threatening even, but I was in such a muddle now that I couldn't have cared less.

He took my arm and escorted me back to the stairs. "You've proved a bit of a nuisance, you know. Especially as everything's coming to a head. Still, I expect the Boss'll put you in the picture soon."

That sounded odd, even to me. Talking about The Super like that. My mind was turning over the possibility that we'd been misled, and that Crichton was not the criminal hit man we'd been led to believe.

Why, I wondered, had everything been made so complicated? Because you're a bleeding pest Pippsy that's why, I told myself.

We got back to Jack and Mags, and although I knew I'd get some harsh words from my husband, it was almost worth it, to see his face when Crichton followed me through the door.

"Now, you three, I'm only going to tell you this once. Don't budge from this room. Particularly you," he gave me a hard stare, worthy of the Super.

"Don't worry," Jack said. "She won't be going anywhere, that I guarantee."

Half an hour later, I was red of face and ashamed. Mags looked distinctly uncomfortable. Jack had given me the most comprehensive telling off of my life.

What had I been thinking of? Couldn't I keep my nose out of the affair? Didn't I realise that I had probably broken umpteen laws? Suppose Crichton had not turned out to be kosher? I could've been killed, couldn't I?

And on, and on and on. I felt the size of a worm when he finally finished. I knew it was because he loved me (I hoped), and worried about me.

I opened my mouth once or twice to tell him how sorry I was, and that I wouldn't ever do anything again without telling him first, but he was definitely not inclined to listen. In the end I just sat there and took it.

When all was quiet at last, Mags ventured, "Did that man, Crichton was it? Did he say that the Super would come and see us when he came back?"

Jack nodded without speaking. He was probably resting his voice.

The WPC had brought coffee, while I was out of the room. I was quite glad to gulp down a cup. It wasn't half bad, I'd drunk much worse.

We must have sat there for another half an hour at least. I began to wish I'd availed myself of the loo after all. Shouldn't have drunk the coffee so quickly.

The WPC came back for the coffee tray.

"Is there anything else?" she enquired.

"Yes," I said, "I really must visit the loo."

Jack looked at me in disbelief.

"No, really and truly this time," I told him.

Mags chipped in, "I wouldn't mind going either."

"Well, alright then," he said. "I'll come with you, and we'll take it in turns."

The WPC looked from one to another of us. Her expression said it all. What sort of new perversion is this?

We trekked along the corridor. Mags and I went first. Then Jack. As he went into the Gents the look he gave me would have rooted me to the spot, even if I'd been inclined to try anything. Which I wasn't.

Back in the interview room, we sat and twiddled our thumbs for another half hour or so.

Then we heard shouting. Mags turned pale. "That's Dave, I'm sure of it."

There was silence, then more shouting and some screaming. More silence.

The suspense was killing me. I longed to open the door and look, but I didn't dare. Jack however, decided the time for action had come. He strode across the room, opened the door and stepped out into the corridor.

I galloped across after him. "What's going on? Can you see anything?"

He turned and glared. "No, I bloody can't."

He stayed there for a few minutes, then closed the door and sat down again.

Suddenly, the door flew open and Crichton stood there.

"Come with me please, the Boss would like to see you."

We trooped into the corridor and off to the Super's office.

As we filed in, the Super stood up. He pointed to three chairs grouped in front of his desk. Once we were settled, he nodded to Crichton, who proceeded to open the drawer of a filing cabinet and produce a bottle of whisky and some glasses. After which, he quietly left the room.

I'd seen this sort of thing on T.V. cop shows, but never expected it to happen for real.

Although scotch isn't my favourite drink, I was grateful for it. I noticed Mags sipping happily, and as for Jack, he almost smacked his lips.

"I suppose," the Super began, "that you would like to hear what's been happening?"

We nodded eagerly.

"I regret to inform you, my dear," this was directed at Mags, "that your husband is now in custody, along with your friends Julia and William Roberts. They will be taken to London shortly, under close arrest. I fear that they will make copious attempts to incriminate you, so I would suggest that you take the precaution of telephoning your solicitor without delay."

Mags looked as if she were about to pass out. She rallied however, and replied, "Yes, of course. Perhaps you could provide me with a phone. I had to leave my mobile behind."

"Certainly, dear lady. A phone will be at your disposal, as soon as I have finished talking to you."

He did the steepling of the fingers bit, looking at the ceiling.

"I think it would be best if I gave you the overall picture. It may take some time and it's very late, so I think it would be advisable if we left this until the morning."

We all looked at him, then I said, "But where shall we go for the night? All our gear seems to be scattered about the county, and it's a bit far from The Flowerdew."

He sighed very slightly then pressed a switch on the equipment on his desk.

In a few minutes the young W.P.C. appeared.

"Give this young woman, your requirements and she'll retrieve them from the hotel. As for sleeping arrangements, I'm afraid we're a bit Spartan here, but you're welcome to make use of our sick bay and showers. Oh yes," he added, as our jaws dropped in surprise. "We're very up to the minute in Cheltenham. The facilities have proved invaluable several times."

So, for the first and I prayed the last time in my life, I spent a night in a police station.

Chapter Thirty-Three

The next morning, after a fairly comfortable night, complete with fresh clothes, and breakfast in the canteen (of which Jack had availed himself to an embarrassing degree), we were ready to face The Super again.

He began pretty much where he'd left off the previous night.

"Now then," he said, settling back in his chair.

"For some time combined police forces here and abroad, have been on the trail of a massive counterfeiting operation. It began in France, moved to the Nederlands then crossed the Channel. The leaders were very careful. It was difficult to pin them down. As soon as we were closing in, they moved their production to a new area. The only hope we had, was to introduce some undercover officers into the mix, which of course we did. I myself was co-opted, somewhat to my surprise."

He paused here, looking reflective. "It's been a few years since I worked undercover, but I have to say, I've found it most exhilarating."

I said, "But surely your work is very exciting? I mean catching criminals, and working out who's done what to whom etc.?"

He looked at me. "My dear young lady, a Superintendant's work is often desk based, and as such, reliant on the information passed on by officers in the field. I missed being 'on the job' as we say, so I grasped the opportunity to be in the thick of things with both hands. I'm nearing retirement, so it was a final throw of the dice for me I suspect."

His lean lined face took on a look of what I can only describe as regret. In that moment he became an ordinary human being.

"Well, well, I won't dwell on that," he said. "Some of the best officers in the country were involved in getting to grips with the perpetrators. A couple of whom, I'm sorry to say, were discovered and summarily dealt with. However, one very brilliant young officer, of your acquaintance, has managed to infiltrate and keep these men blissfully unaware of his identity and his goal. I'm speaking, of course, of Mr. Crichton. Not, I'm sure you realise his real name. I think he successfully kept you completely bewildered as to his objectives."

We nodded in agreement.

"He will, eventually, be moving on to other cases, when he has finished his reports and observations on our current operation."

Mags had been very quiet, but now she said, her voice breaking, "What will happen to Dave? I know I said I was glad to be out of it, but he's my husband, and in spite of everything I still love him."

The Super's expression softened. "At this stage my dear lady, it is not possible to say with any certainty, but I'm afraid that the likelihood is that he will be detained at Her Majesty's pleasure for a goodly number of years."

As quickly as I could, I broke in and asked, "Have you arrested everyone that was at the mansion?"

"As far as we are aware, there are only a few people remaining, with whom we would like to have discussions."

"The honeymooners," Jack and I chorused.

The Super looked a little taken aback. "What honeymooners?......Ah, I see. The couple who were posing as such, of course."

We waited. As there was nothing forthcoming, we felt sure that we were right.

The Super looked at the ceiling then went on, "I must warn you that everything, and I do mean everything that has been said in this room, goes no further – ever!"

He looked at us very sternly.

Jack said, "I can assure you Superintendant, that our lips will be sealed. If there is one thing that we've learned in our business, it's how to keep shtum." I nodded vigorously.

There was one thing further I was desperate to know, so I asked, "Mags's husband had contacts in Europe. Have they been caught?"

The Super's lips twitched. "Be assured Mrs. Standage," he said, "our colleagues in Interpol have been like ourselves, very busy indeed. I'm sure that at some stage something will be leaked to the media, but remember, don't believe everything you hear from those sources."

He stood up. So that was that presumably, and we could go. It was a bit of an anti-climax, but then, the ends of cases were often like that.

In quite courtly fashion he opened the office door, and shook hands with us. Mags was pointed in the direction of the phone, then there we were, not knowing quite what to do next.

As we waited for Mags I said, "I suppose we should get back to The Flowerdew." Jack nodded without speaking.

Presently Mags came back, rather red-eyed.

"I think we should pack up and go home," I said.

"I'll drive us back," Mags said, almost sadly.

We made our way to Mags's car. "I think I shall get rid of this," she told us. "It reminds me too much of Dave. A nice little mini will do me very well."

As we drove off she said, "I'll have to stop for petrol soon, but unless you guys need anything, could we get straight back?"

A couple of miles down the road we spotted a petrol station, with convenience store attached.

We swung in, and to our surprise, considering that it was mid-morning, it was completely deserted, except for one vehicle parked by the side of the store.

"Allow me," my gallant husband said, getting out and proceeding to unhook the fuel line.

While he filled up I looked around the forecourt, and peered at the convenience store. It was very quiet indeed. I couldn't even see an attendant at the cash point.

Jack walked over to the store and pushed open the door. I watched him looking around for assistance. He disappeared out of sight for moment, then suddenly reappeared followed by two people very close behind him.

"Oh, Oh, Mags," I gasped. "It's the missing persons – the honeymooners. Dear Lord, what next!"

Jack and the couple approached the car. The man opened the driver's door and pulled Mags out. "Get in," he said to Jack.

The woman meanwhile grabbed Mags's arm and pushed her into the back seat. She got in beside us, as her companion jumped into the front passenger seat.

He had that nasty looking gun in his hand. "Don't anyone try anything," he said. "We're going to take a little trip. Not far. Just far enough, to where you won't be any further trouble."

My stomach was at it again, dropping below shoe level. Just when we'd thought it was all over. Had they been in wait for us, or was it pure chance?

I had to know. "How did you find us?" I asked.

"We've been waiting around," the woman told us. "After all," she said to Mags, "you're car isn't exactly nondescript, is it?"

"Why didn't you just disappear?" I said.

The woman grinned. "You know our faces. End of story."

Mags seemed to be having trouble swallowing. I knew how she felt.

Jack was being urged along. I heard, "Put your foot down, we haven't got all day."

The man seemed to know exactly where he was going. We twisted and turned, racing through villages, and really opening up on dual carriageways.

Finally we turned off the road along what seemed to be a track. At the end stood a farmhouse, complete with yard and barns. It looked totally deserted, and that didn't bode well I thought.

The man was the first out. Waving the gun he said, "Get out and over to the house."

The woman took an arm each of Mags and I, and pushed us towards the door. It had an ordinary Chubb lock, for which she produced the key. The door opened and we were thrust inside. Jack and the man followed.

He flicked a switch and a dim light revealed a dingy hall, with one or two doors leading off. The place looked as if it had been empty for years. Which it probably had, as it was cold as charity, and filthy.

Mags looked on the point of passing out. I took hold of her arm, and gave it a squeeze.

"It'll be alright," I murmured, with a confidence that I didn't feel.

The woman must have heard me, because she gave a snigger. The man opened one of the doors, flicked on a light and jerked his head to indicate that we should go in.

It appeared to be a cellar, as there was a short flight of steps leading down. The key was turned in the lock. I couldn't believe it was happening to us again.

Through the gloom we could see piles of rubbish. Surprisingly, there were a couple of ragged chairs, and a stained rug on the floor. The origin of the stains didn't bear thinking about.

I tried not to make too much contact with the wall. Anything could have been skulking amidst the piles of boxes and papers.

Jack was pulling his lip, and pacing about.

I looked at Mags thinking, if she doesn't sit down soon, she'll drop down. Poor soul, it wasn't enough that her husband had been revealed as a probable killer, but two of his gang were still on the loose and looked intent on polishing us off.

I examined one of the chairs, and thumped the seat. A thick cloud of dust flew up. However, as it was only dust, I felt that it was safe for Mags to sit on.

She half collapsed onto the chair, and put her head in her hands. I joined Jack and whispered, "Got any ideas?"

He said, "As a matter of fact, yes." It was music to my ears.

"What are we going to do?"

"Hang on, hang on, give me a chance," he said. "It seems to me that our friends are bent on making a run for it. I have a feeling that they're here to meet someone. It can't be Dave or the other two, so it's got to be somebody we don't know. Maybe someone they didn't catch from the mansion, or maybe someone who was never there."

I wondered if he could be right, but somehow, I felt it would be someone that we did know. But who was anyone's guess.

Jack continued. "If Mags really does have some skill at martial arts, we've got to get her up and fighting, I know they've got a gun, but still there's three of us and only two of them."

It made sense, but I was a bit out of my depth when it came to putting the boot in. The nearest I'd ever got to any fighting, was pillow fights at sleepovers when I was a kid! Still, we'd got to think of something.

Jack turned to Mags and said, "Can you really do this martial arts lark? 'Cos it might be a bit useful."

She looked up at him then gave herself a little shake. "I'm actually not bad. Not black belt standard or anything, but not bad. I reckon I could hold my own in a pinch."

That sounded more like it. Jack was already looking around for, I presumed, suitable weapons.

After probing the depths of some rubbish, he came up with a sturdy plank of wood.

"This is the ticket," he said triumphantly. "Now, here's the plan. They're going to come in eventually, probably mob handed, so we must be ready. I'm going for the legs of whoever's first through that door. If it's the woman – too bad, I'm not acting the gent on this occasion. Mags, you leap on the other one and do whatever it is you do. Pippsy, try and lay hands on the gun, because I'm pretty sure they'll come in brandishing it. Now have you got that?"

We nodded, although Mags looked anything but comfortable with the idea of leaping on someone.

We settled down to wait. A drink of some kind wouldn't have come amiss I thought.

My next thought was that a loo wouldn't have come amiss either. Oh dear, I wished I hadn't put that idea in my mind.

Mags whispered to me, "I really need a pee, what shall I do?"

"I need one as well," I told her. "I'll ask Jack to turn his back, and we'll just have to go in the corner."

We found the darkest, dirtiest bit of the room that we could, and Jack obligingly turned away.

As we stood up sighing with relief, I spotted what looked like a table top leaning against the wall. I moved over to have a look.

"Jack," I said excitedly. "Look at this."

He turned round and came over.

"My godfathers," he said, "this is a cellar door. Probably from the days when there was a coal shute, let me have a closer look."

Sure enough, it was a cellar door. Between the three of us we wrestled it open.

Joy unconfined, it let out onto the farmyard. We scrambled out, getting even more filthy in the process, but who cared. I was past worrying about how I looked.

Mags's car was parked by the gate, but to reach it we'd have to cross the yard, and that was in plain sight from the farmhouse. I thought, even if we can get to it, the keys probably won't be in it.

We crept carefully along the wall keeping low. I peeped through the window as we crawled under it. They were both there. She was talking on her mobile, and he was sitting on an upturned box smoking a cigarette.

We didn't hang around. A swift dash over to the car, still keeping as low as we could.

Mags opened the car door. "Thank the lord, I've got a spare key," she whispered.

We were about to climb in, when there was the sound of a car engine approaching. We flung ourselves flat on the ground.

The car swung in through the gate and pulled up. The front door opened, someone got out and opened the rear passenger door.

We heard a murmur of voices, then the farmhouse door opened and the voices became louder.

The woman was gabbling something about being very late, and the others had been nabbed, but they'd caught those interfering b......! I assumed the latter was us.

I raised my head a fraction and caught a glimpse of the visitors. One was a heavy set man with a shaven head, a typical thug I thought. The other was Jeavons, and was obviously very much in charge. So much for the doddering butler.

He snapped an instruction to the thug, who went back to the car and opened the boot. Jeavons was talking to the man and woman. I couldn't hear what he said, but they didn't look happy.

They all disappeared inside, and very cautiously we stood up and got into the car.

I hadn't realised, of course, but luxury cars of this kind don't have anything as mundane as an ignition key that has to be turned.

Mags pressed the brake, then a button on the dashboard, and the engine purred into life, almost silently.

She pushed her foot onto the accelerator, and we almost leapt through the gate. There was no messing around, we were down that apology for a drive at top speed. I found my teeth were clenched, as were my hands. I glanced at Jack, who was sitting next to Mags. His teeth were clenched. All I could see of Mags was the back of her head, but I guessed her teeth would be clenched too.

Suddenly Jack shouted, "Whoa, whoa, we've got to remember exactly how we got here. I don't know about you two, but I wasn't paying too much attention to road signs on the way."

Mags slowed down immediately. We looked back the way we'd come, luckily not too far, and made a note of anything on the road that would act as a landmark.

If we were trying to make our way back to the Cheltenham police, it was a lost cause at that moment. I had no idea which way we should turn. We seemed to be in a maze of twisting lanes, which lacked any signage other than names such as 'Flowerpot Street' or 'Maizey Turnip Lane'.

"This is hopeless," Jack said. Mags pulled over and stopped.

But brilliance will out.

I said, "You've got Sat. Nav. haven't you? Well, we can work it out. Finding Cheltenham won't be that difficult. Then just reverse the route." I sat looking pleased with myself.

Mags and Jack gave me a round of applause. Well deserved, of course, and within minutes we were on our way again, listening to a charming voice dictating every inch we took.

Chapter Thirty-Four

As we pulled up outside the Station, I wondered how the Super would view this latest development. Still, he must surely congratulate me – well us – on formulating a plan to find the last three pieces in the puzzle.

Only problem that I could see was that they'd probably discovered our absence, and taken off.

Which was the Super's take on our latest adventure.

He did congratulate us though, but only on our seeming ability to escape from captivity. I almost said that we were getting plenty of practice.

Before we knew it, we were bustled out to the car by Hawkesley, or perhaps it was Perkins.

"I'm going to ride with you," he said, "and you will be followed by the rest of our team. We're going to nail these b......s, begging your pardon ladies, so that you can sleep soundly in your beds again."

I beamed at him, whoever he was, and we set off.

After half an hour or so, I spotted a turning named 'Candlegrease Bottom'.

"There, there, turn down there, I remember the name particularly. It doesn't matter what Miss Received Pronounciation's saying. It was before we switched her on anyway."

"You're right," Mags chimed in. "I remember it too. That farmhouse is only a short distance from here."

We stopped, and our gallant companion jumped out and ran back to the following car.

He raced back and jumped in saying, "We keep going until we find the turning, then we pull over, and you wait in the car."

"Oh no," I told him. "Every time we do the waiting in the car lark, somebody climbs in and takes us hostage. So, no go I'm afraid. Where you go – we go, and that's that."

I thrust out my chin and dared him to argue. In fact, a look of admiration crossed his face.

"I don't know what my Boss will have to say about it, but I'm game anyway." We came to the opening that led to the farmhouse, and turned in very slowly. I saw that the other car was still parked there.

"They've got to be here," Jack and I chorused.

We stopped and the other cars arranged themselves behind us, effectively blocking any escape attempts.

There were three in total, with the Super in the leading car. Then there was a flurry of activity.

In total eleven officers sprang out and surrounded the farmhouse. I noticed that one or two of them had weapons, and all were clad in protective jackets.

I was out of the car and into the bushes before you could say 'Nessun Dorma'. Jack and Mags were none too tardy either. We crouched well down and waited.

There was a bit of shouting from the officers. It was quite exciting, much more so than the activities at the mansion.

I heard, "Come out with your hands where we can see them," and "Don't try anything, we've got you surrounded." Straight out of a TV crime show.

There was a long pause then the front door opened very slowly. The woman appeared, and to my horror, I saw that the man had a gun in her back. Of Jeavons and his thug, there was no sign.

Oh lordy, I thought, they're probably creeping round behind us at this minute.

The Super called, "Don't be foolish, you can't get away, let the woman go." The man just kept pushing her along. She didn't seem too worried, so I wondered if it was a plan they had.

That's it, I thought, they keep everyone busy while Jeavons makes his escape.

The Super must have had the same idea, because he suddenly shouted, "That's it, go for the house."

There was a concerted rush, in which the man and woman were knocked aside. She fell quite heavily, and started screaming and crying that she was injured, and it was police brutality. No one took the slightest notice

In minutes she and her man friend were cuffed and being led to a van which had just appeared behind us.

We stayed quietly in the bushes, waiting for developments.

Although there was lots of activity in the farmhouse, there was no sign of either Jeavons or his minder (if that was what he was).

After a while I needed to stand up for a stretch. Jack however, gave me a sharp slap on my leg. When I protested, he hissed, "If you start monkeying around again, the next slap will be a hefty wallop."

I subsided, feeling hard done by. Surely something must happen soon, I thought.

The only thing that happened was a general exodus from the farmhouse, minus the other members of the gang.

The gaggle of police stood around talking, while the Super was rattling away on his radio.

Finally he crossed over to our car, and peered in. His face became thunderous when he saw it was empty, but we stood up very quickly and I babbled something about not wanting to be taken hostage in a car again.

He cast his eyes Heavenwards and barked, "The chances of your being taken hostage, as you put it, would have been somewhat slight, seeing as there was nowhere for your car to go."

Put like that it did seem ludicrous, as we were boxed in by police vehicles. All the same, I thought, I didn't feel like being a sitting duck again.

"We might as well get back to Cheltenham," he went on. "Somehow or other the missing persons have eluded us. We'll be back tomorrow to mount a thorough search of the area."

I gawped at him. What an extraordinary thing to say. 'Missing persons eluded them'? 'Back tomorrow for a search'?

We climbed into the car.

"Shall we make our way to The Flowerdew?" I heard Jack ask.

"Yes, Mr. Standage, that would probably be best. Just try and avoid trouble if you can possibly help it. I have undertaken enough high speed journeys recently to last me for the rest of my life. I'm tired out." The Super did sound rather weary.

All of a sudden I felt on the point of collapse. More than anything, I wanted a stiff drink, a hot shower and a cosy bed.

Jack was saying, "We'll be able to get some grub when we get back to the hotel."

Mags said, "Yes, I must say I do feel a bit peckish now."

I closed my eyes in exasperation. Well, I thought, whatever you two are planning I know I'm going straight up to our room, and that's that.

The vehicles behind us had moved off, so Mags started the car and followed them.

The journey back to the hotel seemed endless, although it was only about half an hour. As we pulled up outside, I wondered if my legs would carry me up the steps.

Mags had come to life, big time. Chattering on about the car business, how she was going to plan her life, and how her solicitor was going to work flat out for her.

Jack didn't say much, just, "Really!" "D'you think so." Or, "Yes, you're probably right."

Robert was sitting at the Reception desk as we trailed in. He leapt to his feet saying, "Mr. and Mrs. Standage. Mrs. Carter, how are you?" So that's Mags's surname, I thought.

Robert was going on, "What's the latest on all the dreadful things that have been happening?"

One or two guests came into the hall, agog.

The Barnsworths (I would always think of them as that) wanted to know if we were recovered from our ordeal. That should be ordeals, I thought, grinding my teeth.

"I'm afraid we can't tell you anything it's all very..." Mags began, but Jack interrupted saying, "That's because we don't know anything, of course."

Mags looked as though she could have bitten her tongue out.

"Yes, it's because we don't know anything." Her face was scarlet.

"Sorry, guys," I said in a vague general direction, "I'm going up to shower and go to bed, I'm worn out."

"Can we get you anything?" Robert was all managerial efficiency.

"A large G and T would go down a treat," I said, and headed for the stairs.

"I'll be up in a second," Jack called. At that moment, I really couldn't have cared less. Bed, bed, bed, was all I could think of. Despite having slept reasonably the previous night.

It's relief, I thought. Even Jeavons and his thug still being on the loose couldn't have fazed me, I was so exhausted.

Although it was only seven o'clock, our bed had never looked so welcoming. I stripped off and whipped into the shower, then climbed in with a sigh of contentment.

I'd just closed my eyes when there was a tap at the door. Bother, I thought, that'll be my G and T. For two pins I wouldn't have answered, but Mum had taught me to be polite. The door was unlocked so I called, "Come in."

As soon as the door opened I knew something wasn't right. I resigned myself to the seeming inevitable. In came one of the waiters bearing my drink, closely followed by Jeavons's thug.

How on earth he had managed it I couldn't even guess. But on reflection it occurred to me that apart from Jack, Mags and myself, no one else would have recognised him. Or Jeavons come to think of it.

I sat up in bed and quite calmly accepted my G and T, from which I took a large swallow.

"So, to what do I owe this pleasure?" I asked the plug ugly.

Whether it was my air of nonchalance, or maybe he was naturally thick, so he didn't reply for a few seconds. Then he pushed the white faced waiter to one side, and came up to the bed.

"Someone needs your assistance," he told me.

And I bet I know who, I thought.

"Who would that be?" I said, after taking a sip of my drink.

"My boss," he said. "You won't come to any harm, as long as you do as you're told."

Sez you, I said to myself.

"So, what do I have to do?"

"Get dressed then go for your car. You've got to drive my Boss to the airport." He stood back, with a pleased expression on his face. He'd obviously been carefully rehearsed in what he was to say, and having said it, was awaiting my compliance.

"Which airport was he thinking of?" I responded, taking another sip.

He puckered his brow.

"The Boss'll tell you when the time comes," he said at last.

"Well done you," I said. "I'm sure he'll give you a bonus, for passing on his message so nicely."

Suddenly, I'd ceased to be afraid, or even particularly bothered. I thought, after all I've been through at the hands of this lot, I've had enough.

"You'll have to leave the room," I said, "both of you. I need to get dressed. Can't drive anyone to the airport in my nightie – people might talk."

Honestly, I thought, what's come over me, I sound like some wisecracking dame from an old black and white gangster movie.

It did the trick however, as one, they turned and left. If it hadn't been so serious, I could have laughed myself into hysterics.

There I was alone in the room, the key of the door on my side, plus of course the phone.

I leapt out of bed and locked the door, then grabbed the phone and rang Reception. Caroline's studied tones responded.

"It's Mrs. Standage, don't ask any questions, just ask my husband to come to the phone."

I could hear her draw breath, then call, "Mr. Standage, it's your wife. It sounds urgent."

"What's up Pipps?"

"Don't say anything, just listen. Jeavons and his man have turned up. I had a visit from the thug a few minutes ago, with a waiter and my G and T. I'm to get the car and drive Jeavons to the airport. If you're wondering how I'm managing this call, just be thankful the thug hasn't much between his ears. He and the waiter are outside at the moment, waiting while I dress, if you can believe that. I'll hang it out as long as possible, so that you can get organised. When we come down at least you can tackle the heavy, I don't think he's armed. If you can get the cops over p.d.q. it would help. As to catching Jeavons, we'll have to play that by ear."

There came the sound of knocking and a voice said, "Come on lady, you're not dressing for a Royal garden party."

"I'll have to go, he's getting suspicious. I'm just coming," I called.

"See you in a few minutes." I said to Jack and put the phone down.

I faffed about for a few more minutes, throwing on some clothes and gathering up bits and pieces as if to account for my time.

On opening the door, I almost ran into a fist, clenched to start knocking again I suspected.

"You took your time lady. The Boss won't like that. He won't like that at all."

"Tough," I said airily.

He took my arm none too gently, and pushed me towards the stairs. The young waiter, looking on the verge of a breakdown, was pushed along too.

As we got within reach of the hall, I was told, "Don't try anything. Just walk through."

My eyes swivelled both right and left, looking for Jack. As we drew level with the Reception desk, Robert leapt forward stuck out his foot, and gave a sharp push.

The thug went down sideways with a thump and a grunt. Before he could stand up Robert grabbed a large ornamental vase of flowers from the desk, and crashed it onto his head.

It smashed into a dozen pieces, but it worked. The thug lay still.

"I never could stand that vase anyway," Robert said, without missing a beat. He called over a couple of hovering waiters, one of whom was built like a rugby forward.

"Sit on him," he said, "and if he moves, hit him again."

Although Robert's performance had been impressive, I was distracted. Where was Jack?

I knew I must go to the car. Jeavons had to be drawn out, otherwise we'd be looking over our shoulders for the rest of our lives.

Still hoping to find Jack, I ran down the front steps. Where the hell are you I thought?

Guest parking was pretty well filled, and as I moved along the row of cars, Jack wasn't the only person I was looking for.

I reached our car and pressed the remote. As if that was a cue a hand fell on my shoulder. A man I'd never seen before stood there.

"Who're you?" I asked.

"The man for whom you are going to act as chauffeuse," he said.

"But I thought Jeavons was ...." I tailed off.

"You're very perceptive Mrs. Standage, a little too much so for your own good." The man in front of me was in his late forties, dark haired and hard faced. I could just see a faint resemblance to Jeavons. The disguise had been very skilful.

"Now, shall we go?" he gestured to the driving seat.

"Wouldn't you like to take the car and go?" I said, knowing full well what the answer would be.

"Leaving you here, of course, to give a full description of me to the police. I don't think so." He smiled grimly.

Where was Jack? I was beginning to feel very uncomfortable. It had all seemed so simple when I was in the bedroom.

My heart began to pound. I knew that once we got to the airport that would be the end of me. This man had his escape planned, and I was the final stumbling block to his disappearance.

On shaking legs I climbed into the driving seat. Jeavons settled himself next to me.

"Where are we going?" I asked, trying to control the shake in my voice.

"I'll direct you as we go," I was told, so there was nothing for it but to start up and drive.

As we reached the gate I despaired. Once out on the road, no one would find us. I slowed down, and braked ready for directions. Nothing was forthcoming.

I turned to look at Jeavons. My wonderful Jack was on the back seat, holding a knife at Jeavons throat.

I opened and closed my mouth but nothing came out.

"Don't worry Pipps," Jack said. "Our friends in the force should be here any minute."

Jeavons was looking less than happy. He made to turn his head, but as Jack finished speaking I heard the heavenly sound of sirens.

Jack pressed the knife a little harder into Jeavons's neck.

"You wouldn't really kill me Mr. Standage," he said.

"Try me," Jack replied. "After all that's happened, murders, beatings up, people being kidnapped, it wouldn't upset me at all to draw your blood." He sounded very menacing.

Then, the police were there. Jeavons was invited to step out of the car, formally arrested and cuffed.

Jack got out, and began talking to The Super. I opened my door clambered out, and to my everlasting shame fell in a dead faint.

The next thing I remembered was being lowered onto a couch in the lounge. I then compounded my humiliation by crying my eyes out.

Jack sat down and cuddled me. The rotter was laughing as he said, "Never thought the day would come when I'd have to manhandle you anywhere. Don't cry anymore love, it's all over now, and we're still here."

To which I cried harder than ever.

Robert appeared, bearing a very large G and T and looking concerned and pleased with himself at one and same time.

"Hey man, you're some sort of hero!" Jack said.

"Well, Mr. Standage, I'd had enough of thugs and criminals causing mayhem in my hotel. Now can I get anything else for your lady wife, she's been a first class heroine?"

I mopped my streaming eyes, blew my nose and tried to smile.

"I think I could manage a sandwich if that would be possible," I whispered.

"Say no more," Robert snapped his fingers, and one of the waiters jumped to attention.

"A selection of sandwiches for Mrs. Standage, at the double."

Jack began, "I would quite like......." Robert snapped his fingers again. "And for Mr. Standage also, plus a large single malt, am I right," he turned to Jack, who looked more than grateful.

In bed at last, after consuming three large G and T's and a huge plateful of sandwiches, I felt I could sleep forever.

"We're seeing The Super at half past ten tomorrow," Jack called from the en suite.

"Hmm," I said, and knew nothing more until the sound of "Nessun Dorma" next morning.

Chapter Thirty-Five

Our meeting with The Super was enlightening. The man we had known as Jeavons was a world-wide criminal. Wanted in several different countries.

He had eluded capture for a number of years. Partly due to his moving on when the pursuit got a bit too close for comfort. Mainly however, it was his ability to change his appearance, which at long last had ceased to be a problem.

We were not of course, privy to the man's name, and we accepted that we would never know the extent of his dealings or his identity. The knowledge that we had played a small part in leading to his capture was very satisfying.

It was not enough for me though. I just had to tie up loose ends.

"Who was responsible for the murders?"

The Super gave me a long look. "Somehow Mrs. Standage, I am not surprised that you want 'i's' dotted and 't's' crossed."

As we had suspected, our friends the Honeymooners had been charged with the murders of all three men. We could so easily have been two more on the list. I felt myself break into a sweat at the thought.

"What about the Vicar and his wife, and Eva and her granddaughter?" I wanted to know.

"All of them appear to have recovered from their ordeal. In fact the elderly lady, Eva you said her name was? Well, she is contemplating writing a book about her experiences."

We laughed. That sounded like Eva.

At last, the Super stood up saying, "Well, Mr. and Mrs. Standage, I am very grateful for your, er, assistance in this matter. I'm happy to say that this case has been wrapped up prior to my retirement, to which I am now looking forward."

Jack wanted to know when the retirement would begin.

"I have six months or so, before the day arrives," he said.

"What are you planning to do?" I said.

"Travel a bit, play a little golf, go fishing, spend time with the grandchildren – all the usual things," he told us.

We shook his hand, and wished him a very long and happy retirement. As we reached the door, I couldn't resist, there was one more thing I just had to know.

"Tell me," I said, "did you ever solve the code in the notebook?"

He pursed his lips then to my astonishment, winked and said, "Some of my young officers are still working on that. It's good brain training for them. I shall make use of it, when I retire. I've always enjoyed watching how the fictional guardians of 'Law and Order' operate."

We left the station chuckling.

"He's a wily old bird," Jack said, "I just hope that he doesn't find retirement too dull. Perhaps he'll open a P.I. agency." We laughed, but somehow nothing would surprise me.

Back in the hotel we decided enough was enough. As a holiday it had been an almost complete waste of time, and the thought of home was very appealing.

We packed up and went down to settle our bill.

Mags was in the lounge. She came over, "Forget the bill, but you weren't going to leave without saying goodbye were you?"

We hastened to assure her that nothing was further from our thoughts. I crossed my fingers.

"Come and have a farewell drink. I've got some news anyway."

We were intrigued. Once we were seated, a bottle of champagne was produced.

"What's the celebration?" I asked.

"I've given up on the car dealership idea," Mags told us. "I had a chat with Robert, and we're going into partnership in this hotel. I've got lots of ideas, and Robert's got the expertise. We're keeping some rooms country house style, and making others over, minimalist, and that's just for starters. So I hope we'll see you back here when we have the grand re-opening. There'll be a new name too, we're thinking of calling it 'The Perfect Solution'. What d'you think?"

"We'll drink to that," we said. "Cheers!"